CHRONICLES of the UNICORN KINGDOM

Rise of Neon

Kyle Rawleigh

Kyle Rawleigh

Illustrated by Linda Brisson

CLAY BRIDGES
PRESS

Chronicles of the Unicorn Kingdom
Rise of Neon

Copyright © 2022 by Kyle Rawleigh

Published by Clay Bridges in Houston, TX
www.claybridgespress.com

ISBN: 978-1-68488-021-8 (paperback)
ISBN: 978-1-68488-022-5 (hardback)
ISBN: 978-1-68488-020-1 (ebook)

Special Sales: Most Clay Bridges titles are available in special
quantity discounts. Custom imprinting or excerpting can also
be done to fit special needs. For standard bulk orders, go to
www.claybridgesbulk.com. For specialty press or large orders,
contact Clay Bridges at info@claybridgespress.com.

Dedicated to the best grandparents we could've ever been blessed with — Jim & Terry Rawleigh, Fred & Mary Jo Kreitz, and Peter and Elsie Riehle

CONTENTS

CHAPTER 1

REAGAN

Ever since Liv, Ava, and Claire teamed up with their friend Grace to save the Unicorn Kingdom, things have been very different. Different isn't always a bad thing, though. Let's start with things that are new on Earth where the girls spend most of their time these days.

Liv is a teenager now—she just turned 13 over the summer. She still enjoys learning and school, but she really loves dancing. Her younger sister, Ava, is 11. She is always the first to try new things because she is brave, and she also loves doing anything artistic. Claire is nine, but she is so close to 10 that she can practically taste the double digits. She loves spending time with her big sisters, and her favorite activity with them nowadays is riding unicorns in the secret world they discovered the year before.

The biggest difference in the family is that Claire is no longer the baby. Her parents had another baby, and this time it was a boy. His name is Mason, and he is about six months old. The girls really like how cute he is, but for the most part, all he does is cry and eat. Claire also thinks he is expensive because she keeps hearing her dad say things like "I am never going to be able to retire." Even though their dad jokes about working forever, they are all very glad to have another little family member—even though it isn't a girl.

Another thing that is different nowadays is that "crazy" Grace is their best friend. After finding out that Grace's insane claims about having met a unicorn are actually true, the four girls spend as much time together as they can. Every Saturday night, Liv, Ava, and Claire sleepover at Grace's house. They sleep there because Grace has a treehouse in her backyard, which makes it extra easy for them to sneak off to the Unicorn Kingdom to play with their unicorn pals.

When the girls first discovered the Unicorn Kingdom, they had actually set out to save their dog, Leo. Unicorns have the power to heal, but every unicorn has the ability to use that power only once in their lifetime, so they have to make sure to choose very carefully when they use it. After getting to know the unicorns a little better, the girls learned that there are also many other powers they can be born with. Some have the ability to turn invisible. Some have an incredible power of strength. Others have astonishing speed or powers they use to stun their enemies. A few even have the power to fly. The girls saw all these powers on display last year during an epic battle between two unicorn armies to save the Unicorn Kingdom. After defeating the evil unicorn Neon, they restored the true ruler to power—an amazing unicorn named King Andrew, Claire's unicorn.

After the battle, King Andrew smashed Neon's horn into four pieces and gave one shard to each girl. Now, whenever they hold part of a horn and wish to go to the Unicorn Kingdom, its magic power teleports them there. What is even more fun is that when the girls are in the Unicorn Kingdom, those parts of the horn work almost like magic wands. They are getting really good at using them for magic powers. After King Andrew took back control of the Unicorn Kingdom, there was a ton of work that needed to be done to rebuild it. Neon had made a mess of the place even before the battle.

So much progress is being made there. The unicorns have been working together in order to turn it into the beautiful place it was before Neon destroyed everything. Neon now sits where he belongs in a dungeon below the palace. Everyone else works day in and day out to make the Kingdom a better place to live. That's what the girls do every Saturday night when their parents think they're sleeping in a treehouse. Time passes differently in the Unicorn Kingdom than it does on Earth. Every hour on Earth is about a whole day in the Unicorn Kingdom. So every Saturday night when the girls go into the treehouse and teleport to the Unicorn Kingdom for three to five hours, they actually get to spend three to five days with their unicorn friends in unicorn time.

When they travel to the secret world, they have a nice mix of hanging out and playing with their unicorns, helping rebuild the Unicorn Kingdom, and, of course, having some adventures.

A new adventure was just starting on Earth. It was the first day of school. Luckily, even though the girls weren't the same ages, their school lunchtimes lined up perfectly that year so they could all hang out together for a bit. Liv sat down with a slice of pepperoni pizza next to her two sisters, Ava and Claire. They started talking about how their first day was going when Grace sat down next to them.

"Too bad we have to waste so much time at school when we could be hanging out in my treehouse," Grace said, using her fingers to make air quotes around "treehouse."

"I love the time we spend at the treehouse," Liv said, "but I'm really happy to be back at school. I love my new teacher so far."

"Who is that girl? I've never seen her before," Ava asked as she pointed at a new kid. The girl was Liv's age. She had brown eyes and straight, blonde hair pulled back in a ponytail.

"She is in my class," Liv answered. "She just moved here from Wisconsin. Her name is Reagan." Liv always seemed to know the answer to everything.

"She looks lonely and kind of scared," Ava replied. "Should we go eat lunch with her?"

"I don't know," Claire said. If she's from Wisconsin, she might be a Green Bay Packers fan. Dad says we can't trust Packers fans."

"Who cares what football team she likes?" Grace said. "If anyone understands the feeling of being an outsider, it's me. You guys changed that when we became friends. I think we should go hang out with her."

The girls picked up their lunch trays and walked over to Reagan, who was sitting at a table all by herself.

"Hey, Reagan! My name is Liv. We're in the same class this year. Can we eat lunch with you?"

"That would be awesome," Reagan responded. Even though she looked lonely, it didn't take long to figure out she wasn't shy.

"These are my two sisters, Ava and Claire," Liv said. "The one in the unicorn shirt is Grace. She's our friend."

"Are you a Packers fan?" Claire asked very seriously.

"Of course I am! The only thing I like more than the Packers is dance," Reagan answered. "Thanks for coming to eat with me. I was a little worried it was going to be hard to meet new friends."

"Wait a second. Dad says we aren't supposed to be friends with cheese heads," Claire said.

Reagan started laughing. "Typical Vikings fan."

"Claire, that's rude," Liv said. "Imagine how you would feel if you just started going to a brand-new school, left all your friends and family a whole state away, and then sat down for lunch and kept getting hounded about what football team you liked."

The way Liv was trying to correct Claire made Reagan think about her friends and family back in Wisconsin, and she started to look really sad.

"You should come and sleepover with us at Grace's house this Saturday," Ava said, instinctively trying to cheer Reagan up.

"Really?" Reagan asked with a giant smile on her face.

"Really, Ava?" Grace whisper-yelled at Ava.

"That sounds so fun!" Reagan exclaimed. "I really miss my friends. I will ask my parents tonight, and I'll let you know tomorrow morning."

Right then the bell rang. Lunch was over, and it was time to head back to class. As they were making their way out of the cafeteria, the girls got into their first fight ever.

"I can't believe you invited her to sleep over on Saturday," Grace said angrily to Ava. "You know the only rule is that we can't tell anyone where we are going. Now we won't be able to sneak off."

"Well, if Liv hadn't said all that mean stuff about how sad Reagan must feel, I wouldn't have done it," Ava replied. "I was trying to cheer her up, not ruin our night."

"Well, I wouldn't have said anything if Claire hadn't gotten all upset about her being a Packers fan," Liv said.

"This is Dad's fault," Claire replied.

"It isn't going to kill us to spend one night doing an actual sleepover," Ava said.

"True. I am going to miss Sparkles, though," Grace said sadly.

CHAPTER 2

ROBBED BY GOBLINS

The next day, Reagan was beaming in class right away in the morning, and it was all set. Reagan's parents were perfectly fine with her going to a sleepover. She'd be hanging out with everyone in Grace's treehouse, which meant they were going to miss their first trip to the Unicorn Kingdom since they discovered it.

The rest of the week went by really fast. Saturday arrived before they knew it.

"Later, Mom. We're heading to Grace's for our sleepover!" Liv shouted.

"Sounds good. I'm glad to see you're finally packing light," Mom responded. She was always asking Liv why she packed so much stuff for a one-night sleepover. Liv always told her she liked to be prepared—which was true—so Mom didn't ask any more questions. Even if Liv told her the truth—that she needed Cheetos and apples to feed the unicorns—her mom would have just laughed and assumed she was making a joke.

They biked over to Grace's house. When they arrived, Reagan was already there.

"Well, let's head up to the treehouse for the sleepover," Grace said. She had a fake smile on her face. She tried to seem excited, but it was easy for Liv to tell that Grace was still upset that they weren't going to be visiting the Unicorn Kingdom that night. Since Reagan was new to the group, she didn't pick up on Grace's attitude at all. She hurried out back and started climbing up the wooden steps nailed to the side of the tree that led to Grace's treehouse.

Liv, Ava, Claire, and Grace followed close behind. The four were bummed out to be having a regular sleepover, but as the night went on, they had so much fun that they actually forgot they were missing out on an adventure with their unicorn friends. They were distracted because Reagan was awesome!

They started off talking about dance, which is one of Liv's favorite subjects. Reagan had already mentioned that she liked dance, and the two now found out that they would be dancing at the same studio soon. As the five continued talking, they seemed to just keep finding more things they had in common. On top of sharing so many of the same interests, Reagan was also hilarious. She made Liv laugh so hard that her eyes started watering. Ava's jaw was sore from smiling so hard, and Claire practically had a bellyache from laughing so much. Even Grace forgot she was missing out on spending time with her unicorn, Sparkles.

As the sun went down and the girls ran out of snacks to eat, they finally set up their beds in the treehouse and got ready to go to sleep.

"This is really fun," Reagan said. "Thank you so much for inviting me. I was worried it was going to be hard to make new friends, but you guys are super nice. We should do this every weekend!"

"Totally," Liv said, trying to sound sincere but fully aware that meant they wouldn't be going to the Unicorn Kingdom anytime soon. She never considered that someday she might have to pick between having friends on Earth and spending time with her unicorn, Moonbeam. She didn't want to give up going to the Unicorn Kingdom, but she didn't want to hurt Reagan's feelings, either. She really liked her, and it would be hard to explain why she wasn't invited each time they hung out. As she spent time trying to find a way, she could enjoy both Reagan and Moonbeam, her eyelids got heavy, and she eventually fell asleep. She felt like she had been sleeping only a few minutes when she was jolted awake by Reagan whisper-yelling.

"What the heck was that? Do you guys hear that?" Reagan asked, sounding very afraid.

The rest of the girls were used to sleeping in the treehouse and hearing weird noises sometimes, but then Liv heard a really weird scraping sound below the treehouse.

"There it is again!" Reagan hollered. This time her yelling woke up the rest of the girls. As they woke up, they heard another loud scraping sound. Something was scratching at the bottom of the tree.

"I'll check it out," Ava said as she crawled to the edge of the treehouse and looked down. As she peered over the edge of the treehouse floor, she saw her unicorn friend, Brooke, scraping her horn on the bark of the tree. She was there with Grace's unicorn, Sparkles. The last time the unicorns came to Earth was when they traveled to Andover with the girls to save their dog, Leo. Thinking that maybe the unicorns were just worried about the girls since they hadn't come to the Unicorn Kingdom that night, Ava tried to think quickly on her feet so she could sneak down and talk to them.

"Umm . . . I don't really see anything, but I'll climb down and check it out," Ava said. "Grace, you should come with me."

Grace poked her head over the edge of the floor and smiled ear to ear when she saw Sparkles. "We'll find out what that was in a minute," she said. "It's probably just a raccoon or something. You guys hang tight up here."

Ava and Grace climbed down to talk to their unicorns.

"Thank goodness you're safe!" Brooke said to Ava.

"Of course we're safe. Why wouldn't we be safe?" Ava asked.

"We're not safe? Who are you talking to?" Reagan yelled from the tree fort. Apparently, Ava and Brooke weren't whispering quietly enough. Reagan poked her head over the edge of the treehouse floor and looked down. She could only see Ava and Grace since you have to eat special yellow berries from the Rainbow Jungle in order to see unicorns (it's kind of a long story). The unicorns were completely invisible to Reagan at this time, but she clearly heard a voice she didn't recognize, and it was freaking her out.

Liv peered over and saw Ava and Grace at the bottom of the tree with Brooke and Sparkles. *How am I going to explain this?* she thought to herself.

"Reagan," Liv said. "Every once in a while, we hear animals around here. It's definitely one of the downsides to sleeping outside. It's probably nothing to worry about. I will go down and check it out. You stay here with Claire."

Liv climbed down to find out what was going on. She motioned toward Grace's house to try to get far enough from the treehouse so she could talk to Ava, Grace, and the unicorns without Reagan overhearing. As they got near the house, Liv whispered, "We need to be really quiet so Reagan can't hear us. What's going on? Why are you here?" she asked Brooke and Sparkles.

"We caught word that the goblins were here on Earth trying to recover the pieces of Neon's horn that you have," Brooke told the three girls.

"Hold on! Back up for a minute. Did you say goblins?" Liv asked.

"Yes. Pay attention," Brooke whispered. "Goblins are here on Earth. They're trying to get the pieces of Neon's horn that you have. We aren't sure why, but it seems like they're trying to get his horn repaired for some reason."

"Why would anyone ever want to restore Neon's power?" Ava asked. "He's dangerous, and he's the worst!"

"We haven't figured that part out yet," Sparkles answered.

"Grace," Liv said, "why don't you go up to your room and see if your piece of Neon's horn is still there."

Grace immediately went into her house and ran up to her room to make sure the piece of Neon's horn that served as her gateway between Earth and the Unicorn Kingdom was still there.

"I'm still hung up on the goblin thing," Liv said to Sparkles. "I didn't know there were goblins in the Unicorn Kingdom."

"There aren't goblins in the Unicorn Kingdom, silly. The goblins are in the Goblin Kingdom," Sparkles replied, sounding surprised that Liv wasn't aware of that.

"There is a Goblin Kingdom?" Ava asked, surprised. "What other kinds of kingdoms and creatures are there?"

"Mermaids, trolls, elves, dwarves, and griffins—to name a few," Sparkles said. "There even used to be vampires and dragons!"

"From the stories I've heard, nobody has seen a vampire or a dragon in thousands of years," Brooke said.

Just then, the very surprising conversation about how the Unicorn Kingdom was only a small part of a much larger world was interrupted by a loud scream that came from behind them in the treehouse.

"Aahhh! What was that? What the heck is going on?" they heard Reagan shriek.

"Get away from that! Reagan, help me!" Claire yelled.

Liv and Ava sprinted back to the treehouse and started climbing up. They heard a lot of commotion as they made their way up, and when they got to the top of the steps, they couldn't believe what they saw. There was a green-looking creature tangled up with Claire, trying to pull something away from her.

The creature was a little bigger than Claire but smaller than Liv. Its skin was a dark, shiny green color. It was really skinny and had large hands, long claws, sharp teeth, and pointy ears. Liv and Ava sprang into action, getting in the middle of the fight and trying to get the creature off their little sister. The green creature didn't say anything, but it was snarling as it fought.

"Girls! It's a goblin!" Sparkles yelled from below. "We unicorns can't climb the ladder, but get that goblin down here, and we'll deal with it!"

The goblin continued to snarl and growl as they tried to pull it off of Claire. As Liv tried to pry the creature off, she realized it was very strong, but it didn't seem like it was trying to hurt anyone. It was trying to get whatever it was that Claire was holding. Liv realized that it was Claire's portion of Neon's horn.

"No way!" Liv yelled as she used her dancer's strength and flexibility to kick the goblin right in the face. That startled it enough that the pulling and pushing finally started to work. Claire kicked the goblin in the chest, and it stumbled back toward the edge of the treehouse where Ava gave the final push to topple it over the edge. Hitting the ground didn't seem to slow it down at all, and it got up immediately and darted toward the woods. Brooke had the power of speed, and she took off chasing it. Sparkles stood guard at the bottom of the tree as Grace came sprinting out of her house.

Liv took a deep breath. It felt like the first time she had breathed since she heard Reagan scream a minute earlier. She thought about how scary that just was—how it was probably even scarier for Reagan who had no clue what was going on and couldn't actually see any of it.

"I think we might need to tell Reagan," Claire told Liv.

"It's gone!" Grace yelled as she ran toward the treehouse holding up an empty box she used to hide her part of Neon's horn.

"I'll stand guard until Brooke gets back," Sparkles said at the bottom of the tree.

"Who is Brooke? Who said that? What did Grace lose? What the heck is going on?" Reagan yelled, sounding terrified.

"It's kind of a long story. I guess I'll just start at the beginning," Liv answered.

CHAPTER 3
A MESS MASON DIDN'T MAKE

Liv gave Reagan the short and sweet version of the story. She explained that she knew how crazy it sounded and then told her how they were able to use pieces of a horn from an evil unicorn named Neon to teleport themselves between Earth and a magical place called the Unicorn Kingdom. She explained that goblins were trying to take back the pieces of Neon's horn, and she guessed somebody really bad was trying to repair Neon's horn for some reason.

"I could hear everything, but why couldn't I see anything?" Reagan asked, looking shocked.

Liv explained that the rest of them had eaten enchanted berries at the beginning of their trip, which gave them the ability to see magical creatures that others couldn't see.

"That sounds pretty unbelievable," Reagan said, hinting that she didn't think Liv was telling the truth.

"Come over here," Ava said, motioning to the edge of the treehouse. Ava looked down and saw Sparkles standing guard. Reagan, of course, couldn't see anything.

"Sparkles, can you say something so Reagan will at least hear you and know you're really here?" Ava asked.

"Hey, Reagan! Nice to meet you!" Sparkles said.

"I can't see anything, but I definitely heard that," Reagan said. "Now what do we do?"

Just then Brooke returned from her goblin chase. "That goblin must have climbed a tree or something. I lost it," she said.

"I think we need to stay here at least until morning so our parents don't catch on to anything," Liv said. "Once we leave, we need to go home and check our house to see if the pieces of Neon's horn that Ava and I have are still safe."

"Good thing I snuck mine here!" Claire said. "Hopefully, they didn't get yours, but at least we still have mine!"

"Brooke . . . Sparkles—can you two keep us safe while we try to get some rest?" Liv asked.

"You've got it," Brooke said.

"Let's try to get some sleep. I think we're going to need it," Grace stated.

It took a while for everyone to calm down, and they didn't get very restful sleep after that—especially Reagan. She was half terrified and half excited about what was going to happen in the morning. Eventually, she was able to fall asleep for a very short time.

The minute the sun came up, the scratching noise they heard the night before woke them all up. "Time to get up," they heard Sparkles say.

The girls got out of the treehouse and went straight to their bikes. They rode back to Liv, Ava, and Claire's house with Grace, Reagan, Sparkles, and Brooke following behind. It was pretty easy to sneak the unicorns around so early in the morning because there weren't many neighbors out walking yet who might hear their hooves. Once they got to the house, Liv told Reagan and Grace to wait in the backyard with Claire, Brooke, and Sparkles while she and Ava went in to see if their pieces of Neon's horn were still there.

Liv and Ava ran upstairs as quickly as they could to the room they shared. The moment they got in their room; they knew they were in trouble. The window was open. That was a bad sign because it was definitely closed yesterday when they left. Someone—or something—had pulled it open and torn a hole in the screen. Their room was a total disaster. Everything was pulled apart. Clothes, blankets, paper, and toys were scattered all over the floor. The drawers from Liv's desk had been pulled out and were strewn all over the ground.

Ava ran to her bed, the bottom bunk. She felt under her mattress where she had hidden her piece of the horn. She couldn't feel anything, so she pulled the mattress off her bed and saw that there was nothing there. Liv looked through the drawers on the floor for her piece of the horn. She had kept it in the lower, right-hand drawer, but it wasn't there.

"This is the biggest mess I've seen in a while," Ava told Liv. "Well, at least it's the biggest mess in a while that Mason didn't make."

"You mean our room or this entire situation?" Liv asked Ava.

"Definitely both," Ava answered.

"Well, you know the drill," Liv told Ava.

Ava ran downstairs to raid the refrigerator for some food. She expected they were going to be gone for a while. She grabbed water, snacks, and some food for the girls to live off of for a few days. As always, she grabbed a five-pound bag of Honeycrisp apples to share with their unicorn friends and a bag of crunchy Cheetos to feed King Andrew.

Liv dug through her closet hoping to find what they called their SUSK, a code they used for Secret Unicorn Survival Kit. As she dug through the closet, she was glad to see that the goblins who raided her room the night before hadn't found the SUSK. She pulled it out and looked through it to make sure everything they might need was there. There were matches, a flashlight, extra socks for her and her sisters, and dog treats for Leo. They normally used the rest of the space for food and water.

Liv and Ava ran downstairs and started loading the food into the SUSK. Ava ran to find Leo when they heard their baby brother, Mason, start to cry. Usually, all the crying from the baby drove Liv crazy. She was so focused on getting ready for their adventure that she had almost forgotten he was there. She was glad to hear him cry; that way she knew her little brother hadn't been kidnapped by the goblins.

It wasn't long before their mom was up and coming downstairs with Mason.

"I'm surprised to see you here so early," Mom said to Ava, who was running upstairs with Leo.

Liv grabbed the SUSK and started heading outside, hoping her mom wouldn't see her sneaking out of the house with a few days' supplies. By now, they had done these enough times that Ava knew it was her job to distract their mom while Liv snuck by.

"Oh, yeah!" Ava said. "We had so much fun last night that we decided to spend today together too. We're just grabbing a few things to get ready for the day. We'll be home tonight sometime!"

"Alright, but it's Sunday. You'd better be home for dinner!" Mom mentioned.

Before Liv walked outside, she checked the clock. It was 6:45 a.m. They always had family dinner at 5:00 p.m., so they had a little more than 10 hours (or 10 days in Unicorn Kingdom time) to find out why in the world goblins were stealing back Neon's horn and then find a way to fix it.

"Everyone, gather around Claire," Liv said as she and Ava made their way outside.

Claire stood between Sparkles and Brooke. She had Neon's horn piece in her left hand, which she rested on Brooke. She stretched out her right arm and put that hand on Sparkles. Leo nuzzled up against her legs. Liv, Ava, and Grace each placed a hand on Claire's outstretched arms.

"Reagan, you need to grab hold of Claire if you want to come with us," Liv said.

"Hang on tight, and don't let go!" Claire said excitedly.

Reagan reached out and put her hand on Claire's shoulder.

"I wish we were in the Unicorn Kingdom," Claire whispered, sounding very focused and closing her eyes.

The piece of Neon's horn Claire held in her left hand started to glow. It started dim but continued to get brighter every second. Soon it was so bright that Reagan couldn't keep her eyes open. She closed her eyes and could feel the warmth of the intense glow on her face. Within a few seconds, she could tell the light was starting to fade. She opened her eyes and saw that they weren't in Minnesota anymore. They were in a place she didn't recognize, but she knew it was the Unicorn Kingdom Liv had told her about the night before.

While Reagan couldn't see any unicorns, she could see a beautiful landscape. They were on the edge of an adorable village. She was surrounded by every shade of pink imaginable. She turned around and saw a breathtaking palace.

"Reagan, this is going to be weird for you," Liv told her new friend. "Just stay close to us. You'll be able to hear the unicorns, but you won't be able to see them yet. We're going to talk to King Andrew. He'll know what we should do next."

Reagan listened to what Liv told her and stayed with her friends as they made their way to the palace. She couldn't see any unicorns, but she could hear what sounded like an awful lot of hooves on the ground. She guessed there were probably unicorns everywhere.

The girls made their way through a very large courtyard before going through the grand entrance of the palace. Once inside, Reagan continued to follow her friends until they reached a large room that appeared to have something that resembled a throne at the end of it.

Reagan heard a voice say, "I trusted you four to never tell anyone else about this place."

"King Andrew, it wasn't their fault," Brooke said. "The outsider was with them when they were attacked by goblins, and she found out about us by mistake."

"It was an accident," Liv explained. "This is Reagan. She's our friend, and she came here to help."

"And we brought you Cheetos, Drew!" Claire said.

Liv pulled the bag of Cheetos out of her SUSK and tossed them to Claire, who ran up to the throne and started feeding King Andrew his favorite snack.

"Well, since you brought Cheetos, we'll call it even," he told Claire, smiling.

"We've got a big problem," Liv told King Andrew. "Claire is the only one who still has a piece of Neon's horn. Goblins snuck into our house and stole the other pieces last night."

"I knew I smelled something funny last night!" Leo barked.

"Did your dog just talk?" Reagan asked Liv.

"Oh, yeah, I forgot that part. When he is in the Unicorn Kingdom, he can talk," Liv explained.

26

"I love it here!" Reagan said.

"I'm worried that they're stealing the pieces of Neon's horn to try to heal him for some reason," Liv told the king. "I just can't figure out why."

"That doesn't make any sense to me," King Andrew replied. "We've had peace with the Goblin Kingdom for hundreds of years. I can't imagine why they would break our trust or want anything to do with Neon."

"It's really hard to keep up with all of this," Reagan said. "Is there anything we can do to make it so I can at least see what is going on?"

Just then, Liv's unicorn, Moonbeam, walked in.

"Hey, girls!" Moonbeam said as she trotted up to Liv, who gave her a giant hug.

"Moonbeam," King Andrew said, "please take Liv and her new friend, Reagan, to the Rainbow Jungle. Find Kenji, and get her some enchanted berries so she can see us. If the goblins are trying to restore Neon to power and they already have three out of the four pieces, we need to hurry. Get there. Get Reagan the sight, and get back here as soon as you can. We're going to need all the help we can get. While you guys are gone, we'll decide what our next move will be."

CHRONICLES OF THE UNICORN KINGDOM

Liv grabbed Reagan's hand and pulled her over to Moonbeam. She put Reagan's hand on Moonbeam's side, and then she put her own hand on Moonbeam.

"Don't let go," Liv told Reagan.

"This is *amazing*," Reagan said.

Moonbeam's horn started to glow, and in a few moments, they were in another place that Reagan never knew existed.

CHAPTER 4

ONE FLYING MONSTER AND A CHAT WITH NEON

As Reagan opened her eyes, the first thing she saw was Liv standing next to her. As she looked around, she saw the most enormous trees she'd ever seen. She felt like she was on a different planet. It didn't take her long to realize why this place was called the Rainbow Jungle. The entire sky was the seven colors of the rainbow. Way off in the distance, she saw a mountain that looked a lot like a unicorn horn. She was so focused on taking in the strange, new landscape that she was startled when she heard Liv yell.

"*Kenji! Kenji!* Where are you?!" she hollered.

"You really just yell for him, and he comes to you?" Reagan asked.

"Well, it worked last time," Liv said.

Within a few seconds, they heard something that sounded like flapping wings. Liv peered up toward the tops of the gigantic trees to see if she could spot Kenji, her toucan friend when she saw a creature flying to them that did not look friendly at all. It was large and black. Its wings were much larger than Kenji's.

"Run!" Liv yelled.

"Wait! I think I can actually see it! What is that thing?" Reagan asked.

"We could also see the creatures here before Kenji gave us the berries. I don't want that thing to get close enough for us to find out what it is," Liv said.

Reagan bolted, trying to escape whatever scary creature was flying toward them.

"No! Not that way! You're going the wrong way!" Liv shouted as she jumped on Moonbeam's back.

Reagan didn't stop. She kept running. As she ran, she looked over her shoulder and could see the monster getting closer. It looked like a panther with bat wings, and it was closing in on her fast. Liv was riding on Moonbeam's back, and it didn't take them long to catch up to Reagan. It looked to Reagan like Liv was floating in mid-air because she still couldn't see Moonbeam.

"Grab my hand!" Liv shouted as she reached out.

Reagan grabbed Liv's hand and jumped up as Liv pulled. Reagan landed on the back of a unicorn she couldn't see as Moonbeam darted through the Rainbow Jungle trying to outrun this terrifying, flying cat.

"Moonbeam!" Liv said. "It's time to turn invisible. Reagan, this is going to feel weird. Just don't make a sound."

Instantly, Liv disappeared. Reagan could still feel a unicorn underneath her, but as she looked down, she couldn't see her own body either. She was completely invisible. She followed Liv's instructions and kept quiet. The creature landed on the ground. It clearly couldn't see them, but it started sniffing around. It could definitely smell them. As its nose inched along the ground, it got closer and closer. Just as Reagan was about to scream,

Moonbeam used all her might to kick with her back leg. Her hoof caught the monster right under the chin. Then she landed a unicorn back-leg, upper-cut kick, and the monster dropped to the ground.

"That was a close one," Liv said. "This place has some really freaky things living in it. Let's find Kenji and get out of here."

• •

As Liv, and Moonbeam were trying to help Reagan get the ability to see unicorns and the other creatures that lived around the Unicorn Kingdom, the rest of the gang was trying to figure out what to do next.

"It sure seems like someone is trying to restore Neon's power. I just can't understand why anyone would want to do that," Ava said.

"Has anyone tried talking to Neon yet?" Claire asked.

"We've tried talking to Neon every day since he was put in that dungeon, but he has never said one word to us since we locked him up," King Andrew said.

"I want to try. Could someone bring me to him?" Claire asked.

King Andrew led Claire to a part of the palace she had never seen before. Most of the doorways in the palace led to another room or up staircases, but King Andrew brought her to a stairway that went underground.

"He's down there," King Andrew said. "I don't think he's going to say a word to you, but I wish you the best of luck."

Claire started walking down the staircase. It was very dark and damp as she made her way down the stone steps and toward the dungeon. She could only see because there was a torch burning about every 15 feet. As she got to the bottom of the stone stairway, she began to see cells with bars that looked somewhat rusted. All the cells she walked by were empty. This was clearly a place that didn't get used much anymore.

At the end of the long, underground hallway were two unicorns standing in front of a cell. They appeared to be guarding it. As Claire got closer, she could just barely see the dark outline of Neon's body huddled in the back of the cell with his head facing the corner.

"King Andrew sent me down here to talk to Neon," Claire said to the unicorn guards. "Could you two give us a minute?"

"You know as well as we do that this unicorn can't be trusted. We'll wait at the bottom of the stairway, but you can only have five minutes with him. If you need help, yell," one of the unicorns said as they started walking away.

As Claire looked at Neon lying helplessly in his dark cell, she couldn't help but feel bad for him, even though she knew that a prison cell was where he belonged.

"Neon, I know you probably don't want to talk to me, but my name is . . ."

Neon cut her off. "I know who you are. Your name is Claire. You and your human friends ruined the kingdom I built, and you four are the reason I've been locked in a dark cell since the battle."

At least he is talking to me, Claire thought to herself. Her mom had taught her that people—and probably unicorns—are responsible for their own actions, so she stuck up for herself.

"Actually, I am not the reason you're in here," Claire said sternly. "*You* are the reason you're in here. You are an incredibly powerful unicorn, and if you would have just used your powers to do good instead of scaring everyone to do what *you* wanted, you might have made a good king."

"You're right," Neon said.

Claire wasn't sure what to expect when talking to the evilest unicorn in the history of the Unicorn Kingdom, but she definitely didn't see that coming.

"Obviously, I have had a lot of time to think in here," Neon began. "I regret what I did. I wish I could have a second chance to do things differently. I'm not sure how my powers could have been used to make the world a better place. I've thought about that a lot. How could the ability of mind control and the power to alter memories help anyone? I used to think I was blessed with that power, but the longer I have sat in this prison, the clearer it has become that my powers are a curse."

Now Claire was starting to feel bad for Neon. Her dad had always taught her that people deserved second chances, but there is no way they could ever trust a unicorn this strong who had done so much bad in the past.

"Maybe you can start helping now, even from your cell," Claire told Neon.

Neon let out a laugh that sounded completely evil, and it reminded Claire of who she was dealing with.

"And how might I do that?" he asked.

"Goblins broke into our house last night and stole three pieces of your horn. You must know why they did that, and if you tell me, it will definitely help," Claire told him.

"Really? I have no idea who would have done that or why," Neon told Claire, although she wasn't sure she could believe him.

"Has anyone ever come down here and talked about breaking you out of this dungeon?" Claire asked.

"No. Unicorns have come and tried to talk to me, but you're the first person I've spoken with," Neon said. "I truly don't know why anyone would do this. Maybe it was a loyal member of my old army. I told you that I regret what I did. If you find out who stole the pieces of the horn, send them to me, and I'll gladly tell them to stop. I hate it in this cell, but I belong here."

"Well, I'll keep my ears open, and if we can find out who it is, we'll send them down to talk to you," Claire told him.

"You should check with General Gorum," Neon replied. "He's the ruler of the Goblin Kingdom. I don't know why they're doing this, but if anyone does, it would be him."

"Thank you," responded Claire. "When I find out what is going on, I'll come back and tell you, alright?"

"I'll believe it when I see it," Neon replied.

Meanwhile, back in the Rainbow Jungle, Liv and Reagan were still wandering around with Moonbeam, trying to track down Kenji. While Liv wasn't positive where Kenji was, she was sure she wasn't going to do any more yelling. That flying panther was terrifying, and it got way too dangerous for her liking. Since she was somewhat familiar with the Rainbow Jungle, she decided it would be smartest to head to the cave where Kenji had first introduced them to King Andrew.

Liv thought this was their best plan for two reasons. First, the cave that King Andrew had lived in was the last place she saw Kenji. Second, that's where they were when Kenji brought the girls the enchanted yellow berries the last time they were here. She figured that if they made their way to that cave, even if they couldn't find Kenji, they might be able to find the berries.

With the scary creatures that roamed this jungle, it was probably best to go quietly instead of quickly, so they took their time and tried not to make any sound. Liv got turned around a time or two, but eventually, they made their way to the cave where she had last seen Kenji. The bird she needed was nowhere in sight. As Liv tried to think up a new plan, she heard some flapping wings. It sounded like it was coming in their direction.

"Quick! Get in the cave," Liv whisper-yelled.

Because Reagan couldn't see Moonbeam, she crashed right into the unicorn and got knocked on her bottom. Moonbeam gently bit Reagan's shirt and dragged her into the cave as Liv ran in right behind them.

Liv was relieved when she looked outside and saw a bird instead of a flying panther. Kenji landed on the ground and started hopping toward the cave.

"Welcome back," he squawked, just like the last time Liv had seen him. "How can I be of service?"

"Hey, Kenji! Any chance you could track down some more of those magic yellow berries? I need my friend Reagan to be able to see unicorns," Liv explained.

"Sit tight. I'll be right back," Kenji answered.

He flew off, and just like the last time, he was back in a few minutes with a yellow berry about the size of a strawberry dangling from a branch he held in his beak. He landed on the ground and hopped over to Reagan. She plucked it off the branch and popped it in her mouth.

"Wow! That is really yummy," Reagan said.

"Just wait," Liv said, remembering what had happened to her next.

Suddenly, Reagan made a face that told Liv the tasty snack switched from sweet to sour. Reagan kept chewing. Once she finished it, she saw the fuzzy outline of a creature take shape next to Liv. The longer she stared, the clearer it was until she could finally see the unicorn she had been wandering around the Rainbow Jungle with. And she was beautiful.

Moonbeam had a white body with purple hooves. Her mane and tail were a combination of light blue and dark blue. She had dark blue earrings, beautiful blue eyes, and a purple ribbon on her tail. There were three blue, shooting stars by her front leg.

"Nice to see you, Moonbeam," Reagan said.

"We need to get back to the Unicorn Kingdom. Hopefully, King Andrew has decided what to do next," Liv said.

Everyone thanked Kenji as he flew away. The girls each put a hand on Moonbeam. Her horn started to glow as she teleported the trio back to the Unicorn Kingdom.

The three reappeared in the throne room just as Claire made her way back from speaking with Neon.

"Neon doesn't know who is doing this or why," Claire said. "It seems like he has changed. He actually seems sorry."

"He's probably trying to trick you, and it sounds like it worked," Ava said. "You know we can't trust him, right? We're all safer with him locked away down there."

"He said that if we find out who is doing this, he will tell them to stop," Claire responded. "He also said that if goblins are responsible for stealing three pieces of his horn, someone named General Gorum would know about it."

"Then we need to go talk to him," King Andrew said. "Does everyone agree?"

"Absolutely, but it isn't going to be easy," Moonbeam replied.

"True," King Andrew said. "Grace, I want you to stay here with Sparkles and Reagan. You're in charge while I'm gone."

"Really? That sounds awesome. I'll take good care of everything," Grace said as she skipped toward the throne. "Grace, the queen of the unicorns," she whispered to herself happily.

"Everyone else, pair up and let's get moving. We have a long way to go," King Andrew said.

Claire jumped on King Andrew's back. Liv hopped on top of Moonbeam, and Ava teamed up with Brooke as she always did.

"Leo, you're coming too," King Andrew said.

"Booyah!" Leo hollered in excitement as the girls' three unicorns took off running.

CHAPTER 5

A SHORTCUT THAT SAVED ZERO TIME

The girls rode on the backs of their unicorns as they traveled to the Goblin Kingdom in hopes of speaking with General Gorum. They needed to find out why the goblins were stealing Neon's horn pieces. They rode for so long that Leo got tired. Since King Andrew was the biggest and the strongest, Leo hopped on his back with Claire and rode with them until they reached the mouth of a very large cave at the base of a huge mountain range.

The mouth of the cave was tall and wide. It was very dark inside, but from what they could see at the entrance, it went down underneath the mountain. At the entrance, the downward slope was steep, but not too steep to walk on safely.

"Isn't there another way we can get there? Nothing good ever happens in spooky caves," Claire said.

"Umm, didn't you meet me in a cave?" King Andrew asked.

"Good point. You win this one, Drew," Claire answered.

"The only other way is to climb over the mountain range. Since it gets so cold up there, it will be safer for us to go this way," King Andrew said as he started walking into the cave.

They were probably about 20 steps in when it was so dark that they couldn't see anything. King Andrew used his powers to get his horn to glow brightly. Moonbeam and Brooke did the same, and the dark cave was instantly bright enough to see clearly. The light brightened up the path for quite a distance. They could see far, but Liv could tell they were going to be wandering around for quite a while before they came out the other side.

Leo hopped down because the unicorns weren't running anymore, but the girls continued to ride. Everyone was quiet. They couldn't see or hear anything that sounded dangerous, but the cave was so dark and spooky that they kept feeling like something might be lurking around. They finally came to a place where the cave split. They had to pick whether to go to the right or the left.

"Let's try to listen and see if we can hear anything—maybe the wind or a breeze or something," Liv suggested.

Everyone listened intently. It was very quiet, but they could hear a faint sound. It was very hard to tell what it was, but they decided it was coming from the tunnel that went to the right. They agreed to go that way first. The sound was slowly getting louder as they moved through the cave. Then they came to another split. It was getting easier to hear the sound now, and it was definitely coming from the left. It was still hard to tell what the sound was, but Liv thought it kind of sounded like rushing water. She was hoping that it was the sound of a river or a waterfall at the end of the long tunnel they were in.

The unicorns used the glow of their horns to check both directions. To the right, the tunnel appeared to be straight and long. The glow of their light couldn't reach far enough to see where it either ended or curved. The tunnel to the left where the sound was clearly coming from went straight and then made a pretty sharp curve that they couldn't see around. Since it appeared to curve in the direction they wanted to go and the sound was clearly coming from that direction, they went to the left. As they made their way around the curve, the sound got louder, and they could tell they were getting closer to whatever was making all the noise. The odd thing was that even though they were getting closer to the sound, the glow of their horns helped them see that there was a dead-end ahead.

"Hmmm. You all hear that, right?" King Andrew asked. "We're definitely going the right way to follow the sound, but the tunnel ends ahead."

"We're already here," Ava said. "Let's at least go to the end and check it out. That sound is coming from here for sure. Maybe there is a hidden tunnel or something."

As they moved forward, they saw that Ava was right. In front of the dead-end was a hole in the floor. As they stared at it, they heard the sound coming up out of the hole.

"Maybe we need to drop down there," Liv said. "Let's check and see how deep it is."

The girls hopped off the unicorns and carefully inched their way over to the hole to see how far down it went. As they poked their heads over the edge, the sound became the loudest and the clearest it had been since they started following it. When the glow of the unicorns' horns lit up the area, they could see that it went down much farther than they could jump. It was a sheer drop, so there was no way to climb down. The light also illuminated what looked like eyes—hundreds of them that seemed to be staring at them. Whatever they were started climbing straight up the walls toward them very quickly, almost like they weren't even affected by gravity.

Great! Liv thought to herself. *We weren't following the sound of wind or water this entire time. We were following the sound of scary cave creatures.*

Her thoughts were interrupted when King Andrew shouted, "Trolls! Run!"

The girls hopped on the backs of their unicorns and sped off as hundreds of what were apparently trolls climbed out of the hole and chased after them. Leo followed close behind as the unicorns backtracked to the area where the tunnel forked. They went the opposite way this time. The group moved as fast as they could down the long tunnel. They didn't look back to see how many trolls there were, but the grunting and growling sounds they were making sounded like there were hundreds of them, and they weren't far behind.

The unicorns ran straight for a short while until the path made a curve to the left. They made it around the curve, hoping to see the light at the end of the tunnel, but the unicorns slammed on their brakes before they crashed into a wall. They were at a dead end, and they could hear the hundreds of trolls closing in fast.

"Get ready to fight," King Andrew said.

"There are too many of them!" Brooke responded. "All we're going to do is drain our power and take out a handful of them. They outnumber us a hundred to one!"

Usually, Liv was the one who made the plans, but this time, Claire was the one to think quickly with the precious seconds they had left.

"Liv, take this and keep it safe," Claire said as she tossed her piece of Neon's horn to her oldest sister. "Get invisible with Moonbeam. Stay hidden, and bail us out later."

Liv caught the fourth and final piece of Neon's horn. Right after she had it in her hand, Moonbeam turned invisible because Liv was still sitting on her back. Just as they disappeared, hundreds of trolls poured around the corner. They were smaller than an adult human but a bit taller than Liv. They weren't as skinny as the goblins were. They had a little more meat on their bones. Their skin was a light blue color, and their hair was dark blue. Some of them had earrings and necklaces made of bones, and all of them seemed to have tattoos.

Within seconds, they were overwhelmed by the number of trolls that had them pinned at the cave's dead end.

"You shouldn't have come here," one of them sneered.

Leo jumped out in front and started barking furiously at the trolls. "We can take them!" he hollered.

"Leo, there are too many," King Andrew told him. "We need to surrender and live to fight another day."

"We didn't mean any harm," King Andrew said to the trolls loudly so they could hear. "We surrender."

The trolls swarmed around King Andrew, Brooke, Leo, Ava, and Claire, and started pushing them back out of the tunnel they had just run down. Luckily, because Liv and Moonbeam were invisible, the trolls never knew they were there. The trolls started marching out with their new prisoners. As they were walking, Liv heard one yell, "Snacks!"

Then another yelled, "Snacks!"

Before long, there were hundreds of trolls marching through the cave chanting, "Snacks! Snacks! Snacks!" With so many of them yelling, the sound was deafening.

Luckily, they were so noisy that it made it very easy for Liv and Moonbeam to follow behind. They were still invisible, and the trolls were so loud that they couldn't hear Moonbeam's hooves on the hard cave floor.

The trolls backtracked to the first fork in the tunnel where the girls and the unicorns had decided to go to the right. The trolls went in the opposite direction. It looked like they had gone the wrong way from the very start. They followed the trolls as they wound through the cave for what felt like a very long time until Liv saw the light at the end of the tunnel she had been waiting for.

She had been in the tunnel so long that she couldn't tell if this was the end of the tunnel or if they had worked their way back to the entrance where they had started. As the hundreds of trolls poured out of the cave, they were still chanting, "Snacks! Snacks! Snacks!" When Liv and Moonbeam finally got back out into the natural light of day, they could see that they were definitely not in the same spot where they started. They were in the middle of a camp that belonged to the trolls. The trolls loaded Leo, Ava, and Claire into a cage. King Andrew and Brooke were too big to fit into one cage, so they each had their own. The trolls continued to chant as Liv tried to think of a plan.

Liv had to find a way to save her two little sisters, Leo, Brooke, and King Andrew before Moonbeam ran out of power—and before they became troll food.

CHAPTER 6

BREAKFAST ON THE RUN

Once everyone was locked up, the trolls finally quit doing their "snack" chant.

"I am going to bust out of here, and you trolls are going to be sorry!" Leo hollered.

"We should eat the loud furry one first," a troll croaked, referring to Leo.

"Did you smell that thing?" another troll added. "There is no way that will taste good."

"Let's start with the unicorns," one replied.

"Yes, unicorns are delicious," another troll said. "We should turn them into a stew."

"Everyone knows that unicorns taste best cooked over an open fire," a fourth troll argued.

All the arguing was making it really hard for Liv to think, especially since every word that came out of the trolls' mouths referred to eating her friends and family. *Mean . . . and also yuck!* Liv thought to herself. As Liv listened to dozens of trolls continue to debate over who to eat first or how they should be cooked, Liv finally had a plan or at least part of one.

"I wish my voice sounded like a troll's," Liv whispered while holding the magic piece of Neon's horn. The horn glowed, and all Liv could do was hope her plan worked.

"We should eat them for breakfast!" Liv yelled. Her own voice freaked her out. She sounded like an angry, male troll.

"Breakfast?" a troll asked. "Why would we wait that long? We're starving now!"

"There are two reasons we should wait," Liv said in her scary, troll voice. "The first reason is that everyone knows that unicorns taste best fried with a side of toast. Plus, if we wait a little longer, we'll be hungrier, which will make tomorrow's breakfast even more satisfying."

"That sounds delicious. That is a good idea," a troll answered back. "Gork! Take the stinky, noisy furball to the Goblin Kingdom marketplace, and trade it for bread. Goblins will eat anything, and I'm sure you can find someone who will give us actual food."

"Right away, sir!" a troll responded. He must have been the one named Gork. The troll walked over to the cage that held Ava, Claire, and Leo. Ava and Claire stood between Gork and their dog to protect him.

"No way are you taking Leo," Ava said.

Gork opened the cage door, and Ava ran at the troll full speed, swinging her arms wildly and trying to hit him. Ava's bravery did catch the troll off guard, but he was stronger and tossed Ava aside with ease. Seeing Ava get pushed around made Leo very angry.

"Don't you dare touch them!" Leo yelled as he sprang out and jumped on Gork, trying to bite him. Within seconds, several other trolls ganged up on Leo and stuffed him into a very small cage.

"If those goblins don't eat that thing, they can probably use it as protection. That thing is vicious," a troll said as it locked Ava and Claire's cage.

The small cage they crammed Leo into was stuffed in the back of a wagon that Gork started to wheel away.

Liv's plan to buy herself some time did not go how she had hoped. But she had at least bought herself until morning to save Ava, Claire, Brooke, and King Andrew. She also knew that if Gork was going to try to get to the Goblin Kingdom to trade Leo for bread, they probably weren't too far away from

General Gorum. Liv was completely torn about what to do. She definitely had to wait for the trolls to fall asleep in order to save everyone—everyone except Leo, that is. All she could do now was wait to rescue everyone else and hope they made it to the Goblin Kingdom in time to save her dog.

Moonbeam and Liv snuck away from the troll camp where they could still see and hear what was going on, but they were far enough away for Moonbeam to turn off her invisibility power and save her strength.

"What are we going to do now?" Moonbeam asked.

"We wait until the trolls fall asleep, and then we are going to bust everyone out," Liv croaked.

"Liv you need to fix your voice," Moonbeam said.

"Oh, sorry. I wish my voice was normal again," Liv said in her troll voice, using her horn piece to wish her voice back to normal. "Once they fall asleep, you can turn us invisible again to get us near the cages. I'll use the magic from Neon's horn to unlock them," Liv said, her voice sounding normal again.

Moonbeam and Liv tried to remain patient waiting for the trolls to fall asleep. It was really hard to stay calm. Each second that went by made Liv more nervous. She was afraid they weren't going to get to the Goblin Kingdom in time to save Leo. After about two hours of waiting, Liv and Moonbeam saw Gork pushing his wagon, which was now packed full of loaves of bread.

"They loved that four-legged furball. Look how much bread they gave me," Gork said. "He was so ferocious when I dropped him off that they gave me all the bread in the market and said they were going to use him as a guard monster."

"Ha!" a troll replied. "Foolish goblins. They should have eaten it. Let's get some rest, Gork. The sooner we fall asleep, the sooner we'll be up for tomorrow's feast."

Many of the trolls were gathered around large bonfires that burned throughout their camp. Slowly they started making their way into various tents and shelters they had built. Many of the

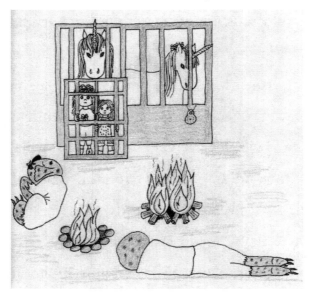

trolls continued to stay around the fires, but they quit adding logs. Eventually, the remaining trolls fell asleep, still lying by their fires as they died out. Once Liv thought all the trolls were asleep, she and Moonbeam started to work out their plan.

"Let's do this," Liv said as she hopped on Moonbeam's back.

Moonbeam turned both of them invisible and started walking slowly toward the cages. She tried to walk as gently as possible so her hooves wouldn't wake up any trolls as she snuck through the camp. More trolls were lying around the cages than Liv realized. Moonbeam had to awkwardly step over some of them to make her way to the cage that held Ava and Claire. They were still awake, and they looked scared.

"Stay quiet, and don't move," Liv whispered. "I'm going to open the locks on all three cages. You two need to get on your unicorns, and then we need to get out of here fast."

Ava and Claire nodded to show that they understood.

"I wish this cage was unlocked," Liv whispered. The lock on the cage clicked and opened. A troll lying near the cage snapped awake.

"I told you to be quiet," it said.

Ava and Claire didn't make a sound, and the troll laid back down and went to sleep again.

"I wish this cage wasn't locked," Liv whispered again. Brooke's cage unlocked. "Don't move until I say to," Liv whispered to Brooke.

"I wish this cage was unlocked," Liv said yet again. With a final click, King Andrew's lock came undone. "Okay. I am going to get the locks off so they can all get out at the same time," Liv whispered to Moonbeam. Liv quietly hopped off her unicorn, and as soon as they were no longer touching, Liv was visible again. She pulled the lock off her sister's cage first. Next, she carefully removed the lock from Brooke's cage and set it on the ground without making a sound. Finally, she inched her way over to King Andrew's cage. She removed the lock. All the trolls in the area were still asleep. She noticed an extra latch on King Andrew's cage. If she didn't lift it, he wouldn't be able to get out. As she lifted it, the old metal made a horrible squeaking sound.

That was enough to wake up the closest troll. As the troll sprang to its feet, King Andrew used his stun power to blast it, and it fell back to the ground. The shot from King Andrew's horn was enough to wake up several trolls around them. "Time to move!" Liv yelled.

Ava and Claire opened their cage right when Brooke and King Andrew pushed their doors open, and everyone was free. But the trolls were waking up and figuring out what was going on. Moonbeam turned off her invisibility power, and Liv jumped on. Ava hopped on Brooke, and Brooke used her nose to boost Claire onto King Andrew's back. They took off running.

"Our breakfast is running away!" a troll yelled.

They were now out in the open instead of trapped in a tunnel, which made it easy for the unicorns to outrun the trolls, especially Brooke who had the power of speed. She cruised around all the trolls with ease, and she was the first one to escape the troll camp. King Andrew and Moonbeam weren't far behind, and it didn't take long for all of them to outrun the trolls.

Brooke slowed down so everyone else could catch up to her and Ava.

"We need to get to the Goblin Kingdom and save Leo!" Liv yelled as they trotted toward Ava and Brooke.

"Good thing we're just about there," Ava said, smiling. In the distance, they could see the Goblin Kingdom. It looked a lot different than the Unicorn Kingdom. There were no shades of pink, homes made out of candy, or a beautiful palace. Even from far away, Liv thought it looked dirty—not dirty like covered in garbage or anything but more like everything was covered in soot. From far away, it looked like they did a lot of work building things, but she couldn't tell what. As the sun started to rise, she could see that most of the structures were tall and black. They almost looked like they were made out of slate.

"Let's go save Leo," King Andrew said as he took off running. In about 10 minutes, they were sitting outside the Goblin Kingdom. Large, black walls made out of some kind of metal surrounded the kingdom. There was a very large, arched doorway with wooden doors. It was clearly the entrance.

King Andrew walked up and kicked the doors with his front foot. "We need to speak to General Gorum," he yelled.

There was silence for about 30 seconds. Just when Liv thought they were never going to be let in, the doors started to open.

CHAPTER 7

GENERAL GORUM

As the massive wooden doors swung open, they saw some goblins, but not as many as Liv had expected. The last time they saw a goblin, it was wrestling Claire, trying to steal the last piece of Neon's horn. None of these goblins attacked, which was a nice change of pace after their run-in with those nasty trolls.

"I am King Andrew, leader of the Unicorn Kingdom, and I need to speak with General Gorum right away," King Andrew declared.

"Also, have any of you seen our dog?" Claire asked.

"What's a dog?" a goblin responded.

"A furry creature that runs around on four legs," Claire tried to explain.

"Oh, we just got one of those," the goblin said. "That thing is vicious. We named it Gladiator. He's protecting General Gorum right now. Follow me. I'll take you to him."

Liv was relieved to hear that Leo was safe. She thought it was funny that a bunch of monsters had named her sweet dog Gladiator. Who would've thought that goblins were nicer than trolls? The girls stayed on the backs of their unicorns as they followed the goblin through the Goblin Kingdom.

They made their way down the streets, and Liv saw that her thoughts about this place were right. It was dirty. Everything seemed to be under construction. They had many very tall buildings, but each one appeared to be in the process of being built even higher. At the center of the city was the tallest tower—the only one that seemed to be completely built. It was black like the rest of the structures and had pointy spires that almost looked like claws coming out of the top. They made their way into the tallest tower. The inside was much prettier than the outside.

The ceiling on the first floor was very high. The floor and walls were all marble, and beautiful pillars were lining the way toward a tall set of stairs. Those stairs led up to a large throne where Leo sat next to the biggest goblin the girls had ever seen.

Liv guessed he was about the height of her dad, probably about six feet tall. It looked like he ate a lot because he had a round tummy. His legs and arms made him look like an overgrown frog. His skin was a lighter shade of green that was covered in dark green spots. He had large ears that were a little droopy. The teeth on his lower jaw were so large and pointy that even though his mouth was closed, many of his sharp teeth stuck out. He wore a brown, button-up coat that barely seemed to hold his belly in. It reminded Liv of a military uniform. He had purple horns and a big crown on top of his head. And he had a very dissatisfied look on his face.

"That's them! They are my family and friends I was telling you about," Leo said to General Gorum.

"I enjoyed you while I had you, Gladiator," General Gorum said to Leo. "But if they are your family, you're free to go."

Leo ran down the stairs, and the girls hopped off their unicorns to give him hugs.

"It has been a very long time since a unicorn has set foot in the Goblin Kingdom," General Gorum said. "What brings you here, King Andrew?"

Everyone walked over to the bottom of the marble stairs that led up to the throne. Liv thought it felt kind of weird talking to someone who was so high above them.

"We came here to ask you why goblins are trying to gather up the pieces of Neon's broken horn," Liv explained. "Neon claims he doesn't have any idea why members of your kingdom would do such a thing, but he thought you might know."

"Yes," General Gorum responded. "We have gathered three pieces so far, and there is one piece that we still need. Do you know where we can find it?"

"We don't understand why you want them," Liv answered. "Are you trying to fix the horn? The unicorn it belongs to is the meanest creature we've ever met!"

"That is true, General Gorum," King Andrew added. "Neon singlehandedly almost destroyed the Unicorn Kingdom."

"I talked to Neon myself," Claire told General Gorum. "He agrees that his power is a curse. He couldn't think of a time when the power to change memories could be used for good instead of bad."

"We aren't trying to destroy the world—we're trying to save it!" General Gorum shouted. "We have a problem, and Neon is the only one who will be able to save us."

The girls exchanged very puzzled looks with the unicorns.

"A few months ago, we received word that a dragon is roaming around," General Gorum said.

"That's impossible. Nobody has seen a dragon alive in hundreds of years," King Andrew replied.

"I know," General Gorum said. "I didn't believe it either, but the elves to the north of us have actually seen it. I don't know why they would lie to me about something like that, but even if it wasn't true, I figure it's better to be safe than sorry. King Andrew, I don't need to tell you how powerful a dragon is, and you know the Goblin Kingdom doesn't stand a chance on our own. Even with our advanced weapons, we're no match for a dragon. Neon's ability to alter its memory or control its mind is going to be our best chance of survival—and I don't just mean the Goblin Kingdom; I mean the entire world as we know it."

"What if you're wrong?" King Andrew asked. "What if the dragon isn't real and we restore power to Neon for no reason? His powers combined with his desire for control are almost as dangerous as a dragon."

"I agree with you that it is a tough situation," General Gorum said. "There are risks to healing Neon's horn, but there are equal—maybe even greater—risks to doing nothing."

Just then the doors crashed open, and the goblin who had led everyone to General Gorum came running in. "General Gorum! It's real, and it is heading toward the city!" the goblin yelled, sounding very frightened.

"Try to calm down. How much time do you think we have?" General Gorum asked the goblin.

"Not long. If you go up a few floors, you'll see it flying this way from the north," the goblin said.

"Everyone, follow me," General Gorum said as he got up from his large throne. "We'll try to see this with our own eyes, and then maybe we can come to an agreement."

General Gorum started heading toward another wooden door, and everyone followed him. He opened the door that led to a stone, spiral staircase that went upward and then started climbing the stairs.

Everyone followed him, and Liv noticed that General Gorum was surprisingly quick for how large he was. They went up what felt like seven stories before they opened another wooden door and entered a large room that was also made of stone. Liv, Ava, Claire, and Leo were all panting from climbing so many stairs. The unicorns and General Gorum didn't seem to be phased by the hundreds of steps they just ran up. General Gorum, followed closely by everyone else, ran over to a large window.

Liv saw it right away, but since it was so far away, it looked very small and appeared to be black in color. She could see what looked like very large wings slowly flapping in the distance. It was so far away that she couldn't tell for sure if it was a dragon or not, but whatever it was, it was definitely heading toward them.

"Well?" General Gorum asked.

"I can't believe it. How is there a dragon alive?" King Andrew wondered. That was the first time Liv had ever heard the king so frightened.

General Gorum reached inside the pocket of his military-style coat and pulled out the three pieces of Neon's horn they had stolen. "I have failed my kingdom. I am too late," he said sadly.

"We don't have a choice," King Andrew responded. "We are going to have to heal Neon's horn and hope he can use his powers to help us defeat this dragon. I'm sorry we can't help you now. For the time being, you and all your goblins are welcome to stay with us in the Unicorn Kingdom. We'll keep you safe, and we can work together to defeat this dragon."

General Gorum turned to the goblin who had informed them that the dragon was coming and said, "Evacuate the city. Tell everyone to bring with them only what they can carry on their backs. Make sure they bring their weapons. I'm afraid we're going to need them. We need everyone in the city to be heading to the Unicorn Kingdom in less than an hour."

The goblin nodded and started running down the spiral staircase. General Gorum was still holding the three pieces of Neon's horn in his hand. Liv walked up to the leader of the Goblin Kingdom and held his other hand.

"We're going to help you," Liv told him reassuringly.

General Gorum handed Liv the three stolen pieces of Neon's horn. She gave Ava her piece and put Grace's in the SUSK. General Gorum nodded sadly and started heading down the staircase.

An hour later, General Gorum was waiting in front of the large wooden entrance doors to the Goblin Kingdom. The girls,

Leo, and the unicorns were standing by his side. In front of him were all the goblins in his kingdom.

"Thank you for moving so quickly," General Gorum told his goblins. "There is a dragon coming this way. It is no longer safe for us here. King Andrew has offered us a safe place to stay. We are going to the Unicorn Kingdom. We'll make a plan there and come back when it's safe."

The goblins stood silently as the large, wooden doors opened. They weren't in love with the idea of leaving their homes, but they seemed to understand that it was for their own safety. Once the doors were fully open, General Gorum turned around and started walking. The girls, Leo, and the unicorns turned and started walking, too, followed by thousands of goblins. As they walked, they heard a terrifying sound—a combination of a roar and a screech. Liv turned her head. She knew the noise came from the dragon. It was still pretty far away, but it would be at the Goblin Kingdom soon. They were leaving just in time.

CHAPTER 8

TALE OF A TORCHED TAIL

General Gorum and King Andrew led the way. They weren't moving very fast since so many goblins were following them. Claire was riding on King Andrew's back so she could easily hear what the rulers of the two kingdoms were talking about.

"How is your relationship with the trolls?" King Andrew asked.

"As good as it can be," General Gorum answered. "We've gotten along fine for a very long time. They come to the Goblin Kingdom on occasion to trade in our marketplace."

"They think we're food," Claire told General Gorum.

"That isn't anything you need to worry about anymore," General Gorum replied. "I will be able to straighten that out.

Once we explain what is going on, you will be safe. They'll listen to me."

Even though they weren't moving fast, it didn't take long to enter the troll camp because it wasn't that far from the Goblin Kingdom.

As soon as King Andrew and Claire got in sight of a troll, it ran back to camp yelling, "Breakfast came back! Breakfast came back!"

The trolls gathered quickly and started running toward King Andrew and the rest of the group.

General Gorum walked between King Andrew and the charging trolls and yelled, "Stop!"

The trolls came to a screeching halt.

"These unicorns, humans, and the four-legged furry monster of fury are under the protection of the entire Goblin Kingdom. They are saving us, and they are not to be harmed," General Gorum said.

"Saving you from what?" Gork asked.

"A dragon," General Gorum answered.

The trolls all laughed hysterically. "A dragon? There is no such thing as dragons," the trolls muttered through their laughter.

Just then their laughter was broken by the terrifying roar of the dragon they had heard earlier. Everyone turned around and saw a large, black dragon circling over the top of the Goblin Kingdom not far behind them. It was shooting flames out of its mouth, setting their city on fire. Liv couldn't believe how bright the flames were, even from a distance. The dragon swooped down, launching fire out of its mouth like a flamethrower. With a few swoops, the dragon had set most of the Goblin Kingdom on fire.

"It's impossible!" Gork yelled.

"The unicorns have offered to keep us safe in their kingdom, and together we'll make a plan to defeat the dragon," General Gorum said.

"You're welcome to join us," King Andrew told the trolls. "I think we could use all the help we can get."

"We'll come with you," Gork said.

The trolls behind him started nodding. They didn't have any more time to talk because they heard another screech from the dragon. Through the smoldering city, they saw the dragon appear through the smoke and start heading toward them.

"Run!" King Andrew yelled.

Everyone took off running toward the tunnel that led through the mountains and to the Unicorn Kingdom. There was a problem, though. The entrance to the tunnel on the troll camp side was nowhere near the size of the entrance on the Unicorn Kingdom side. They had to fit three unicorns, three humans, a dog, hundreds of trolls, and thousands of goblins through the small opening before the dragon got there. It was complete chaos as everyone charged toward the small cave opening.

"Brooke, you need to take Claire! I'll try to slow this thing down," King Andrew said.

Nobody was sure exactly how King Andrew planned to do that, but there was no time to argue. Claire jumped off King Andrew's back and onto Brooke's. Brooke used her speed power and took off running with Ava and Claire. She was one of the first to reach the cave, and King Andrew was happy knowing they were safe. He waited at the back of the group as everyone else tried to push their way through the small cave entrance. They were all moving, but they weren't able to go fast enough. King Andrew saw the dragon closing in and knew he had to try to do something.

"Hurry!" King Andrew yelled as he charged toward the flying dragon. As he ran to face the beast head-on, his horn started to glow, and he used his stun power to try to slow the monster down. He fired a shot from his horn, and the dragon easily dodged it by doing a barrel roll through the air. King Andrew fired again as it got a little closer, and this time there was a direct hit. The only problem was that the blast of King Andrew's stun power didn't even slow down the dragon. It kept flying toward him. It was getting close, and King Andrew saw the dragon open its mouth, which was glowing orange.

King Andrew knew that if he didn't do something fast, he was going to be torched like the Goblin Kingdom. He fired one final stun shot, and the blast went right into the dragon's mouth. It hit the back of the dragon's throat, and then it fell out of the sky. The dragon was so massive that when it crashed to the ground, it tore up the earth and left a cloud of dust as it hit the ground and slid to a stop.

King Andrew turned around and saw the last of the goblins running through the cave entrance. His back was to the dragon, which started to stand up, coughing wildly. King Andrew caught his first glimpse of the dragon, but he didn't waste a lot of time staring at it before he took off running toward the cave to join everyone else. The dragon was enormous up close. Its scales were different shades of black. The scales on its chest were a very dark shade of black. Its face, neck, and front legs were lighter, almost a gray color. Its back legs and tail were a darker black, but not quite as dark as its chest. It had very sharp claws. King Andrew also noticed that it was covered in spikes—spikes on its elbows, chin, and cheeks. It also had large, sharp, dark purple horns on top of its head and spikes running down its back from the top of its head to the tip of its tail.

As King Andrew ran, the dragon took off flying again. The king could hear the enormous wings flapping behind him. He could feel the wind created from the beast's powerful wings that kicked up dust and dirt as they went up and down. He ran as fast as he could toward the cave with the dragon closing in on him. As King Andrew entered the cave, it was dark until he lit his horn. He couldn't see any of the others, which was good—it meant they were far ahead, but he could hear them.

The dragon was too big to get into the cave, but its head fit in. It had a long neck that reached in several feet before its wide shoulders stopped it from entering the cave. It opened its mouth, which was glowing orange again. King Andrew didn't slow down because he knew the dragon was about to breathe fire in his direction. He heard a roar, and the cave lit up behind him. He was running as fast as he could. The cave walls lit up brightly all around him as he tried to outrun the flames. King Andrew felt the warmth creeping up behind him as he charged deeper into the cavern. He had just enough of a head start because the flames behind him were starting to die down. He was just out of reach, but the flames got close enough to catch the end of his tail on fire.

"Hot! Hot! Hot!" King Andrew shouted as he turned and blew his tail out as if it were a candle. Behind him, he heard the dragon roar again in anger. He wasn't sure if the monster was just mad that everyone escaped or if the cave made the roar louder, but it was so noisy that it made his ears ring. The dragon angrily pulled its massive head and neck out of the cave and flew away.

Phew! That was a close one, King Andrew thought to himself as he kept running to catch up with everyone else. He was picking up the scent of his burning tail, but luckily it didn't hurt. He had never seen anything withstand his stun power before. At least he was able to slow the dragon down for a moment. He knew right then and there that Neon was their only chance of surviving. Now they just had to make it back to the Unicorn Kingdom and make a plan before the dragon got there.

The trolls knew their way around the underground tunnel so well that they were able to get to the other side very fast. Fortunately, once they got out, there was no sign of the dragon. When they were back in the light of day, Claire finally saw King Andrew. She ran over to him and gave him a giant hug.

"I was so worried about you! What happened to your tail?" Claire asked.

"I barely got away from it. That dragon is the most powerful creature I have ever seen. We need to get back to the Unicorn Kingdom as fast as we can. Neon is our only chance," he told Claire.

Claire jumped on King Andrew's back as they led their makeshift army of trolls and goblins to the Unicorn Kingdom. Everyone was going as fast as they could, but they were all getting tired. The group made it back just as the sun was going down. By that time, the girls, Leo, and the unicorns hadn't slept in almost two days.

"I'll have Sparkles and the flying unicorns keep an eye out for the dragon tonight," King Andrew said. "Everyone needs to get some rest. Tomorrow we'll come up with a plan."

Normally, when things like this happened, Liv had trouble sleeping. But this time, everyone was so exhausted that they fell asleep almost immediately.

As Liv dozed off, she knew that healing Neon's horn was going to be their best chance, but she couldn't help but worry that by healing his broken horn they might be bringing back the only monster that was more dangerous than a gigantic, fire-breathing dragon.

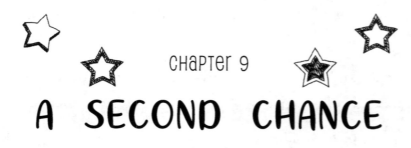

CHAPTER 9

A SECOND CHANCE

The next morning, Liv was awakened by someone yelling her name and gently shaking her shoulder. She was still pretty tired, and it took her a few seconds to wake up and realize what was going on. It was Reagan.

"Liv! This place is amazing!" Reagan said excitedly. "While you were gone, I made another new friend. And guess what?"

"What?" Liv responded, rubbing her tired eyes.

"My new friend is a unicorn!" Reagan exclaimed.

Obviously, Liv wasn't surprised by that since Reagan had just spent about two days in the Unicorn Kingdom surrounded by nothing but unicorns—and Grace, of course—but Liv was still happy for her friend. It's a really magical thing to have a unicorn friend. What could be more fun?

"That's great," Liv said, smiling.

"So," Reagan continued, "I noticed there are hundreds of monsters around here now. What did you guys do while you were gone?"

Liv looked around and saw goblins and trolls sleeping everywhere. She realized it might have been a good idea to explain to Reagan what was going on before they went to bed, but late was better than never. She began filling her newest friend in on what happened—that they were working with the trolls and the goblins to come up with a way to stop a dragon from destroying everything in the world they escaped to every Saturday night.

"So let me get this straight," Reagan said. "We are now an army of trolls, goblins, and unicorns that is going to resurrect the evilest unicorn of all time in order to defeat a fire-breathing dragon."

"Exactly," Liv said.

"That is the craziest thing ever," Reagan exclaimed.

"It is the craziest thing ever so far," Liv told Reagan. "We need an amazing plan. It might sound exciting, but we saw that dragon and it is *terrifying*. We need to be really careful."

By now, trolls, goblins, unicorns, and even some of the other humans were starting to wake up. A unicorn Liv had seen before but had never met was walking toward them. The unicorn had powder blue fur, orange hooves, and a large, orange star covering its left eye. Its mane and tail were a combination of dark blue and blaze orange.

"Good morning, kiddo!" the unicorn said to Reagan.

"Liv! This is the unicorn I was telling you about," Reagan said. Her name is Star."

"Nice to meet you," Liv told Star.

Everyone was awake now, and King Andrew invited the girls, their unicorns, Leo, and General Gorum to his throne room to discuss what they needed to do next.

"Someone needs to heal Neon's horn, and soon," General Gorum said.

"Are we sure there isn't some other way? There has to be another way," Ava pleaded.

"I've thought about that a lot, Ava," King Andrew told her. "I can't see any way that we stand a chance without Neon's help."

"What if he just uses his power for evil again?" Ava asked. "What if he tries to take the Unicorn Kingdom back from you? What if he tries to escape? We've had him locked up in a prison for a very long time. I doubt he is just going to forget about everything and help us."

"You might be right, but he may be our only hope," King Andrew answered.

Ava bit her lower lip and looked frustrated. She didn't like the idea at all, but she didn't have a better plan, and neither did anyone else.

"I think he'll do it," Claire said. "He seemed different somehow when I talked to him."

"General Gorum," King Andrew chimed in. "I think it would be best if you had your goblins and trolls build some defenses to help protect the Unicorn Kingdom. Use anything you need, and don't be afraid to ask for help from unicorns if you need it."

General Gorum nodded and went to gather up the goblins and trolls so they could get to work. From their time in the Goblin Kingdom, Liv knew they were expert builders and were sure to come up with some great ideas to keep everyone safe.

"Now we need to heal Neon's horn. Who is going to do it?" King Andrew asked.

"I'll do it. I'll heal Neon," Star said.

King Andrew led the entire group back to the entrance of the prison. When they got to the bottom of the stairs that led to Neon's cage, Claire said, "We'll take it from here, but you guys stay close in case we need a backup."

Liv, Ava, Claire, and Grace headed down the long, dark hallway that led to Neon's prison. Star walked closely behind them. Once they got to the last cell, they saw Neon still lying helplessly on his prison floor.

"We figured out what is going on," Claire told Neon.

"I'm surprised you came back," Neon scoffed.

"The goblins were trying to get the pieces of your horn so they could fix you," Claire explained. "You were right. We went to talk to General Gorum, and he told us all about it."

"And why would they want to do that?" Neon asked.

"Because there is a dragon, and we think your power to alter memories is our best chance to defeat it," Liv said.

Neon started laughing—a laugh that still sounded completely evil. That didn't help them feel any better about the fact that they were going to fix his horn and set him free.

"Dragons aren't real," Neon said, sounding annoyed. "They're just stories passed down by unicorns over hundreds of years. I shouldn't be surprised that you and your friends who got me locked up here in the first place came all the way down here to mock me."

"We aren't mocking you," Ava replied.

"We saw the dragon, and it's terrifying," Liv told him.

"And we brought the pieces of your horn down here with this unicorn to heal you," Claire said.

Now Neon was roaring with laughter. "We both know that I am going to sit in this prison for the rest of my life. Just do me a favor, and don't bother coming down here again."

Claire pulled out her piece of the horn. Liv, Ava, and Grace did the same, which actually got Neon to stop his evil, maniacal laughing and get very serious.

"We're coming in, and we're going to fix you," Claire told him. "I need you to trust us because we need to trust you."

"I wish this cell wasn't locked," Ava said as she held her piece of Neon's horn. "I never thought the last time I used Neon's horn for magic would be to set him free."

The cell clicked, and they knew it was now unlocked. They worked together to pull the very heavy prison door open.

"I can't believe this is really happening," Neon told them as they approached.

Neon lay on the ground as they walked to him. Each girl held their piece of his shattered horn in place. Liv's part was on the bottom, Grace and Ava's was in the middle, and Claire held the point. Once everything was in place, they told Star they were ready.

"*Once in my life a miracle to make, it is time now for my power to wake. In my soul, I can feel it's time to use my power to heal,*" Star chanted.

As they had seen many times before, Star's horn started to glow the softest, most beautiful shade of pink the girls had ever seen. It continued to glow more brightly until a pink beam shot out of Star's horn directly at Neon's broken horn. Each piece of the horn began to glow pink. The glow was especially bright in all the places it was cracked—the places where King Andrew had shattered it in the battle to save the Unicorn Kingdom. It was the battle to save the kingdom from the very unicorn they were now healing.

In a few seconds, the glow on Neon's horn faded. The girls let go as the large, black horn fused back together and Neon's power was restored. The girls stepped back, afraid of what was going to happen next.

"How can I help?" Neon asked them.

"I'm glad you asked," Liv said with a sigh of relief. "We've got a lot of work to do."

CHAPTER 10
GIANT PINK WEAPONS

Over the next few days, everyone worked very hard to prepare for the fight of their lives. There was a lot of unity among the trolls, goblins, and unicorns. Liv found it hard to believe how quickly everyone came together, especially since just the day before, the trolls were trying to eat her sisters. Even though she was surprised, Liv was very glad it worked out that way.

It took a lot of planning at first, but once the plan was set, things started falling into place very quickly. That also made Liv happy because they had been gone for six days in Unicorn Kingdom time, which meant they had four more days to figure out how to save their secret world and still make it home with her sisters in time for Sunday night dinner.

Liv felt pretty good about their plan. It definitely had some risks, but this was risky business, and there wasn't any way around that. The goblins used their building skills to design some awesome weapons that were going to help them defend themselves. They used wood from trees they cut down in the Unicorn Kingdom to build what looked like giant crossbows. They built five of them altogether. They placed one at each of the four corners of the palace and the fifth one in the very center.

On top of the crossbow-like structures were large, bundled nets. They were made to swivel around in a complete circle so they could be fired in any direction. The dragon was huge, so the crossbows also had to be huge. Whoever was firing the crossbow would sit on top of a circular, wooden deck where the weapon was mounted. It took four creatures—goblins, trolls, or unicorns—to turn it in any direction.

The one sitting on the deck that aimed and fired the weapon could aim the crossbow up and down. So they had to work as a team to get the weapon to work right. The one aiming would have to shout out directions. They agreed to keep it simple. The only commands would be "right," "left," and "stop." Whenever the shooter yelled "stop," those who were turning it would immediately stop so the shooter could aim.

The goal was to fire a giant net through the air to hopefully knock the dragon out of the sky and trap it on the ground.

Whenever a net was fired, the four who were helping turn the structure would jump up and help reload another net. The giant crossbows would have looked very intimidating if they weren't hot pink. That was the color of the trees they had chopped down to build them.

It took a lot of practice, but eventually, they got very good at working as a team. Those who were trained to fire the crossbows got better at launching the nets where they wanted them to hit. Liv wanted to try it out and found she had excellent aim. She was going to be using the one on the southwestern corner of the kingdom. After seeing how awesome Liv was at using the crossbows, Ava wanted to give it a try. She seemed to have a knack for it as well. Her station was the one in the center of the kingdom.

Even though the giant, pink, net-launching crossbows were an awesome invention and a great idea, everyone agreed that it was going to be tough to hit a flying dragon with them. But they agreed that their best chance of winning was to take the fight to the air. While Neon had many strong powers, he obviously couldn't fly, but that was another problem the goblins were able to solve.

The goblins built five harnesses. The first four were designed to wrap tightly around the bodies of unicorns who had the power to fly. On the bottoms of the harnesses, on their bellies, was a large, metal, built-in hoop. Each hoop had a chain that hooked into it. The four chains were about 15 feet long and all led to the fifth harness, which was Neon's. His harness, which also fit tightly around his body, had four metal hoops on top where the chains were hooked.

The device almost worked like Santa's sleigh. The four flying unicorns would line up in front, and the chains on their harnesses would hook to the back of Neon's harness. All five would start running together, and when the four flying unicorns took off, Neon would leap into the air, and they would pull him off the ground and fly him around. This took a lot of practice and proved to be even more difficult to get to work right than the giant crossbows. It got Neon up into the air, but the four flying unicorns could not maneuver very fast. If the unicorns tried to turn, they bumped into each other, fell out of formation, and dropped to the ground. It worked best if they flew slowly and steadily, which wasn't ideal for battling a fire-breathing dragon in the air.

As they practiced flying Neon around, it became obvious that they would need a way to distract the dragon while they positioned Neon in the sky to use his mind control and memory-altering powers on the dragon. Sparkles volunteered immediately for this task, which was the most dangerous part of the entire plan. Several other flying unicorns agreed to work with Sparkles to distract the dragon. They just had to get Neon in position long enough to control the dragon's mind and wipe out its memory.

As for the unicorns, goblins, and trolls, many of them were going to hide inside the palace for safekeeping. It was mainly the younger and older ones who would be inside to make sure they stayed safe. Sparkles refused to let Grace ride on her back because her part was too dangerous. So Grace agreed to stay in the palace and keep all the young trolls, goblins, and unicorns calm.

Everyone else was set up with various jobs. Some were to deliver extra supplies such as giant crossbow nets around the city to make sure everyone had what they needed to stay in the fight. Many of the trolls and goblins covered themselves in makeshift armor and weapons in case the dragon landed inside the palace courtyard and they needed to fight on the ground, but everyone was really hoping that didn't happen.

The goblins also built a wooden water tower in the center of the city—it was pink, of course. The goblins, trolls, and unicorns worked together to carry buckets of water from a nearby lake to fill up the water tower. The unicorns came in handy as they were hooked up to wagons and hauled several buckets back and forth at a time. The water tower had a spigot they could open to fill buckets with water that could be used to put out any fires that started inside the palace walls.

Once everything was built, King Andrew had a meeting with everyone to review the plan once more. Over the years as ruler of the Unicorn Kingdom, he had always found that the best plans were the simplest ones. Many situations rarely went according to plan, and the simplest strategies were easiest to adjust on the fly.

"Remember, everyone," King Andrew said. "All we need to do is get Neon in range of the dragon, and Neon will be able to take care of the rest. We are going to pack everyone inside the walls of the palace, and I mean everyone—every unicorn, goblin, troll, and human will be inside the palace walls."

"Don't forget the dog!" Leo yelped.

"Of course, Leo, you need to be in here with us too," assured the king. "If the dragon sets the homes outside the palace walls on fire, we are going to let them burn. We've rebuilt them before, and we can rebuild them again. The important thing is to keep everyone safe. Let's recap how we do that. Once we see the dragon, Grace will get all the goblins, trolls, and unicorns who are too young or too old to fight safely inside the palace. She will keep an eye on them for us and keep them calm. While Grace is getting them to safety, those manning the crossbows need to get to their stations."

"Or *womaning* the crossbows," Liv reminded King Andrew.

"Right!" King Andrew chuckled. "Fire those nets as rapidly as you can. If you're able to hit the dragon and take it down, that will make things a lot easier for us. I expect it will be hard to hit, but even distracting it will make a big difference. Sparkles and the brave army of volunteer flying unicorns will take off once Neon and his flying unicorns are secured in their harnesses. Sparkles, you and your team will go up first while the others slowly get Neon into position. You *have* to be careful—all of you. This is going to be super dangerous."

"We won't let you down!" Sparkles hollered.

"Once Neon is in place," King Andrew continued, "he will use his power to wipe the dragon's mind clean. We need to control the dragon long enough to trap it. Of everything that is going on, nothing is more important than keeping Neon safe and lining him up to get control of the dragon. Without Neon, we don't stand a chance."

Stomp! Stomp! All the unicorns stomped to show they understood the plan.

"Continue to practice your jobs," King Andrew said. "If everyone does their part, we can win this thing."

Stomp! Stomp! Liv also noticed the trolls and goblins banging the heels of their weapons on the ground or against their armor to go along with the unicorns' stomps.

Everyone continued to practice and drill to get the best they could at their job in preparation for the fight of their lives. Two more days went by, and the girls had now been gone eight days, leaving two days until dinnertime.

On the eighth day, the girls were sitting around chatting after lunch when they heard the sound of a goblin war horn. That was the signal that someone had spotted the dragon. The girls all sprang to their feet and started looking around. Far off in the distance to the east, they saw a small, black, flying figure. Liv knew it only looked small because it was so far away and that there was a massive, fire-breathing dragon in the distance heading straight toward them.

Liv looked around at her sisters and her friends. Ava and Claire had stern looks on their faces. Liv knew they were probably afraid, but they definitely weren't showing it. They had been in situations like this before. Reagan looked excited, and Liv was still worried that her newest friend didn't quite understand how dangerous this was going to be. The girls all gave each other a big group hug.

"Everyone, be careful," Liv said, looking directly at Reagan to hint that she was worried about her. "Keep each other safe. Be smart, and do your jobs. You know what to do!"

With that, everyone took off in the directions they needed to go to make sure the plan worked. It was time to battle a dragon.

CHAPTER 11
A WEIRD WAY TO DEFEAT A DRAGON

While Grace was getting those who were too young and too old safely hidden away inside the palace, Liv and Ava made their way to their net-launching crossbow stations. Ava was in the middle of the city, and Liv was in the southwestern corner as they had been for their last several days of training. As Liv climbed onto the deck of her crossbow, her entire team showed up just behind her. There were two goblins and two trolls who would help rotate the crossbow, based on her commands.

For Ava, things weren't going as well. She was supposed to have three goblins and one troll to help rotate her crossbow, but the troll hadn't shown up.

"He should be here by now," Ava said, worried.

"That troll must have chickened out," a goblin responded.

Just then Ava saw Reagan running by.

"Reagan! Reagan!" Ava shouted. "We're missing a helper. If we don't get another person here soon, we aren't going to be able to aim this thing right."

"I'll go find someone!" Reagan shouted back.

They heard a roaring screech in the east. The dragon was already here. Ava and Reagan saw the dragon blow a steady stream of fire and begin torching many of the unicorns' homes surrounding the palace.

"There isn't time!" Ava shouted. "I need you to do it!"

Reagan jumped into the open spot that a troll was supposed to fill.

"Left!" Ava shouted.

Reagan noticed the three goblins pushing to rotate the crossbow to the left, so she started pushing in the same direction with all her might.

The dragon flew by outside the palace walls. "Stop!" Ava yelled. She squeezed the trigger and launched a giant net in the direction of the dragon. The monster was too fast, and her net flew through the air well behind it. This was going to be much harder than she thought.

The three goblins jumped up onto the deck and started to reload Ava's crossbow. Two goblins pulled the large string back to lock it into place, while the third goblin struggled to get another net loaded. When Reagan saw it was having trouble, she jumped up to help out. She wished she had spent the last couple of days getting trained, but now she was stuck figuring this out as she went. The goblins got the net into place and jumped back down.

The dragon flew by so fast that it almost looked like a blur as it shot out another heavy stream of fire, setting more of the unicorns' homes ablaze. Ava saw more nets flying through the air from the other crossbows, but like her, everyone was having trouble keeping up with the dragon's speed. The shots weren't even close.

The dragon flew around the palace and started blasting fire on the other side of the village, destroying even more of the unicorns' homes. Ava could not believe how fast this monster could destroy things. If they didn't do something quickly, there wasn't going to be a single home left in the village that surrounded the palace.

"Right!" Ava yelled as her team started to rotate her around for a second shot. As Ava was still being rotated, she fired again.

It was closer this time, but the net still wound up going behind the dragon. It was just too fast. This time, Reagan hopped up immediately to help reload. She was getting more familiar with the drill. As they worked to get another net loaded, Ava saw more nets fly through the air, and all of them missed their target. The dragon dove downward again, lighting homes afire on the southern end of the city. Ava's third net was now loaded, but the dragon was flying very high in the sky, out of range of any of the crossbows.

"Where are the flying unicorns?!" Reagan asked.

"We need to do our job and trust that they'll do theirs," Ava hollered back.

Much of the village surrounding the palace was now burning. It felt like this had been going on for hours, but in reality, it had only been a few minutes. Ava's third net was in place as she saw the dragon dive-bomb down like a falcon and start to blow fire at the northern portion of the village. This was a big problem for two reasons. First, the entire village around the palace was now burning in a giant ring of fire. The fire was spreading slowly on its own, which meant they were trapped. Second, the ring of fire that was billowing smoke would prevent anyone from escaping. The smoke was getting thicker by the minute, and if the dragon was outside the firewall it had created, it was almost impossible to see where it was.

Luckily for Ava, even though she couldn't see, she could definitely still hear. She closed her eyes to try to focus on listening. The atmosphere around her was pure chaos. She could hear yelling. She could hear running. She could hear the crackling of the large fire burning outside the palace walls. Hearing all this, her hands started to get sweaty like they did when she was up too high or when a spider was nearby (her only two fears). Then she faintly heard the sound of large, flapping wings that sounded like they were coming from her left.

"Left!" Ava shouted.

The three goblins and Reagan rotated Ava and her crossbow to the left.

"Stop!" Ava hollered when she felt she was in the right spot. Her crossbow immediately came to a halt.

Ava had guessed right. The massive dragon was flying through the wall of smoke headed right for her. She could see that its head was cocked to the side. She knew it was looking at something else and didn't see her. She took her time and aimed carefully. She squeezed the trigger. The sound of the crossbow firing was loud enough for the dragon to hear. The net whizzed through the air right on target, but the dragon saw it just in time and started to move out of the way. The right side of the net caught the spikes of the dragon's tail. Flapping its wings, the dragon hovered in the air as it looked back at the net hanging on its massive tail. With a powerful flick, the dragon easily flung off the net, snapped its head forward, and looked directly at Ava. The partial hit had been just enough to make it mad.

"Run!" Ava yelled. The goblins and Reagan took off running in different directions. Ava hopped off and ran as fast as she could in the opposite direction of the dragon. She peeked over her shoulder as she ran and saw the dragon flying toward her crossbow. It opened its mouth, which started glowing orange. Flames shot out of the creature's mouth as it flew toward the crossbow. Then Ava saw the crossbow completely engulfed in flames. The blast was so powerful that the crossbow didn't just burn—it exploded. Ava turned back around and tried to keep running, but she was no match for a flying dragon that was trying to blast her with fire.

She pumped her arms and legs as hard as she could and then saw the first thing that made her feel hopeful since the fight started. Sparkles and dozens of other flying unicorns were cruising through the air, heading right for her—and the dragon.

The fire was getting so close behind Ava that she could feel the heat on her back. Just then, Sparkles and her friends whizzed past her.

Ava noticed that she couldn't feel the heat anymore, so she turned her head and saw Sparkles and the other flying unicorns zooming around the dragon's face, annoying it the same way mosquitoes annoyed Ava every summer in Minnesota. She looked down and saw fire spreading from where the dragon had just blasted her crossbow.

"Quickly! Put out the fire!" King Andrew yelled.

Dozens of goblins and trolls quickly ran to the water tower and began filling up buckets to put out the fire. Ava looked around to see where her crossbow crew was. She saw two of her goblin friends run over to a goblin that was on the ground, not moving. She saw Reagan heading in that direction, so Ava ran over there too.

The goblin had a helmet on with a big dent in it. It looked like debris from the crossbow must have hit it in the head when it exploded. The goblin was breathing but unconscious. The two goblins picked up their friend and started dragging him to safety.

"Wait!" Reagan shouted. She ran over and pulled a sword from the sheath of the goblin who was unconscious.

"We need to get to Liv. She'll know what to do," Ava told Reagan. They both started running to the southwestern portion of the palace where Liv was still womaning her crossbow.

As Ava and Reagan headed in that direction, they heard the dragon roar very loudly. They looked up and saw that Sparkles and her flying unicorns were doing a great job distracting the dragon. That was when Ava first noticed that the four harnessed unicorns were flying Neon toward the dragon as he hung below them. They were already about halfway there. They were moving slowly, but there was so much going on that it looked like they were going to be able to sneak into position. Their plan was working!

Within a few minutes, Ava and Reagan were at Liv's crossbow waiting for their plan to unfold.

Liv was aiming her crossbow at the dragon. "I can't get a shot without hitting a unicorn," she told Ava.

"Look!" Ava shouted as she pointed to Neon. They could see his horn starting to glow red. The dragon was still trying to shoo away the flying unicorns when the red glow of Neon's horn caught its eye. The monster opened its mouth and launched fire like a bullet in the direction of Neon and the four unicorns who were holding Neon in the air. The four unicorns had nowhere to go but down, and fortunately, they were able to drop low enough to avoid the blast. Unfortunately, the two unicorns on the right side got tangled in the chains. They were flapping their wings, trying as hard as they could to stay in the air, but it was no use. They started twirling in the air, falling downward as they began descending toward Liv's crossbow. They looked like a crashing helicopter as the flying unicorns fought with all their strength to stay in the air, but they just couldn't do it. As they continued to spiral downward, they went right over Liv's head. They flapped their wings just strong enough to clear the palace wall and soften the blow when they hit the ground. Ava could tell that all their efforts to stay up at least made for a softer landing. It definitely still hurt, but the unicorns were going to be okay. Lucky for them, they didn't land in the fire burning outside the palace walls.

Just then, Ava turned her head as she heard the dragon screech. It was flying toward the spot where Neon and the flying unicorns had crashed. It must have known that Neon was their only hope. The evil look in the dragon's eyes as it flew toward them told Ava that it was on a mission to finish off Neon once and for all.

Even with all the chaos going on, Liv had stayed trained in on the dragon. To get to Neon, it had to fly right over her. She waited until the last possible second when the dragon was too close for comfort, and then she pulled the trigger. The net flew through the air. Liv could tell the dragon saw the net. It tried to slow down, but it was moving too fast. The net collided with the dragon's face and surrounded it, wrapping around its wings and turning it into an enormous, black missile. It got so close to Liv's head as it shot over her that she had to duck to avoid getting hit. The dragon crashed into the palace wall, but it was so large and going so fast that it smashed right through the wall, leaving a giant hole and a pile of rubble.

The dragon groaned as it skidded to a halt, trapped and tangled in the net. As it slid to a stop, it thrashed, trying to break free. Neon stumbled to his feet, still chained to four flying unicorns lying on the ground. His horn was now glowing red, and a red, laser-like beam shot out toward the dragon. Liv watched in awe as this unfolded and then got distracted as she saw Reagan sprint through the gaping hole the dragon left in the wall. In her hand, Reagan had the sword she had swiped off of the goblin, and now she was charging toward Neon and the dragon.

"Reagan, no!" Liv yelled, but it was too late. Reagan either couldn't hear Liv or was ignoring her. Either way, she wasn't planning on stopping.

As Reagan reached Neon, she could hear the unicorn gritting his teeth.

"It's too strong!" Neon said.

"Don't give up! We're all counting on you," Reagan said.

Neon's front legs gave out as he dropped to his knees, but the red beam never let up as he tried to wipe out the dragon's memory and take control of its mind. The dragon was surprisingly still. It barely moved, and its eyes were faintly starting to glow red. It was working.

"I can't do it!" Neon hollered, almost as if he were in pain.

"You have to!" Reagan reassured him.

Just then, Neon toppled onto his side, and the red beam coming from his horn stopped.

"I didn't finish it. I don't think I completely wiped out its memory," Neon struggled to say. He was clearly exhausted.

The dragon was still trapped in the net, lying almost completely still with its eyes glowing red. It started to blink, and Reagan could see the red start to fade from its eyes. It closed its eyes and shook its head a few times, and then the red glow was gone. The dragon stood up in the net and again tried to break free.

"No!" Reagan yelled as she charged at the dragon with the sword.

Liv, Ava, and Leo all took off running to try to stop Reagan, but she was too far ahead.

The dragon used its large front talons to slice through the net, and it was free just as Reagan was running toward the beast screaming like a crazy person.

"Aagghh!" Reagan yelled as she charged fearlessly at the dragon.

The dragon crouched down on all four of its legs. It bared its teeth as Reagan charged, and as it exhaled, smoke came shooting out of its nostrils. As Reagan lifted the sword above her head, ready to swing with all her might, the dragon tilted its head to the side like a confused puppy and said, "Momma?"

"What?" Reagan yelled in surprise as she stopped and dropped the sword.

"Momma!" the dragon yelled as it used its giant nose to nuzzle Reagan.

"What the heck is going on?" Reagan asked, looking confused and uncomfortable.

"This is going to be bad." Neon said as he struggled to his feet.

CHAPTER 12

GENERAL GORUM'S CROWN JEWEL

Liv and Ava were the first to reach Reagan as the monster scooped her up and seemed to be hugging her.

"What is it doing? What did you do, Reagan?" Liv asked in confusion.

"I don't know," Reagan said as the dragon was gently smothering her in a dragon hug. "I was charging at this thing, and just as I was about to whack it in the head with this sword, it called me Momma, and now I think it's giving me a hug."

Liv vaguely recalled learning about this in a science class at school. When baby ducklings hatch from an egg, they think the first living being they see is their mother. Maybe that somehow happened with the dragon.

"Neon, how much of that thing's memory did you erase?" Liv asked.

"I'm not exactly sure," Neon answered. "It was so strong that I had a hard time telling if the job was done or not."

"Momma!" the dragon bellowed as it held Reagan in its arms.

"This is super weird," Reagan said.

"Reagan, I think Neon did better than he thought," Liv said. "I'm pretty sure he erased the dragon's memory so far back that it thinks it's a baby again. And—I think it imprinted on you. I'm pretty sure this dragon thinks you're its mom."

Ava started laughing hysterically. "You've got to be kidding me."

"Put me down!" Reagan yelled.

The dragon immediately put her down on the ground and sat on its bottom. It used its two enormous front hands to cover its eyes and then started crying like a baby.

"Sorry, Mom," the dragon said between sobs.

Reagan looked at her friends, confused. Then King Andrew rode up with Claire on his back. "What's going on? Did it work?" he asked.

"Kind of," Reagan told King Andrew. But instead of a fire-breathing, flying monster of destruction, we now have a full-grown dragon that thinks it's a baby. And it also thinks I'm its mom."

"What do we do now, Neon?" King Andrew asked.

"Don't look at me," Neon shouted. "This was your plan. I did my part. I thought you had it all figured out from here."

"Maybe if it thinks Reagan is its mom, she can teach it to be nice," Liv wondered.

"It's worth a shot, and it's as good of an idea as any," King Andrew said.

"We've got about a day and a half before we need to get home for dinner," Liv said. "We can start cleaning up this mess while Reagan trains her dragon."

"I don't know how to train a dragon," Reagan said, sounding nervous.

"I don't think you have much of a choice," Ava told Reagan. "Do you have a dog?"

"Yes," Reagan answered, not exactly sure where Ava was going with this.

"Well, it will probably be easier than training a dog because this dragon can talk. I'd start by trying to teach it not to burn things—or eat us," Ava said.

"Come on, everyone. We need to get this fire put out," King Andrew said.

Everyone made their way back to the palace to start getting buckets of water to douse the flames. As they walked away, they heard Reagan yell, "Are you guys seriously just going to leave me here with this thing? I already told you that I don't know how to train a dragon!" As Reagan tried to get someone to help, her new, giant, baby dragon sat next to her sobbing uncontrollably.

Eventually, Reagan was able to get the dragon to stop crying. She started working with it on basic dog commands such as sit, stay, and rollover. The dragon was actually a pretty good listener, and Reagan quickly found out that it was too big for the roll-over trick. It did a great job rolling, but it smashed a lot of stuff in the process.

After a while, the dragon started to grow on Reagan, and she decided to name it George. Every time she noticed her dragon's mouth start to glow orange as if it were going to blow fire, she quickly corrected it and told it no. That led to many more giant tears rolling down the dragon's cheeks since it did not like Reagan scolding it.

While Reagan continued to work with the dragon, everyone else was trying to put out the fires outside the palace. They worked through the entire night. As the girls worked with their army of trolls, goblins, and unicorns, they were able to get everything to stop burning. There was a lot of work to do to repair the palace and the village surrounding it, but at least everyone was safe.

As night turned to morning, Liv realized they were going to have to leave soon. She had been so wrapped up in the mess with the dragon and cleaning up the disaster of the battle that she hadn't even thought about the fact that they no longer had pieces of Neon's horn. She was sure a unicorn could probably teleport all of them back home, but she was suddenly very sad that they wouldn't be able to return to the Unicorn Kingdom anymore whenever they wanted to.

That evening, King Andrew called a meeting in the palace with all the trolls, goblins, unicorns, and Leo. Everyone was there except Reagan who was still dragon training somewhere outside.

"I want to thank everyone for a job well done," King Andrew announced. "Our plan worked, and it is incredible what we were able to accomplish when we worked as a team. Everyone did their part, but I want to extend a special thank you to Neon. We all thought you weren't capable of doing anything good, but you proved us wrong. You were brave and selfless. You are *never* to use that power again without my approval, and if you're willing to accept that, I will pardon you."

Neon was silent at first. "You'll give me a second chance?" he stammered.

"You've earned it, and you have earned my trust," King Andrew said.

"I won't let you down," Neon replied.

"Then it is decided. Neon will no longer be locked in the dungeon. As long as he uses his powers with my permission to do something good, he is free."

Stomp! Stomp!

The stomping was interrupted as they heard Reagan yelling from above, "Wahooo!"

Her dragon landed in the middle of their meeting, and Reagan was riding on its back. "George has come a long way," Reagan proclaimed. "He is a great listener. I've got him trained not to set things on fire anymore."

Reagan covered the dragon's ears and whispered to everyone else, "I also trained him to only eat vegetables. Keep feeding him veggies, and he'll be happy. He won't bother anyone. Also, I should warn you that we do not have the potty-training part down yet."

Reagan uncovered George's ears and said, "Let me down." The dragon lowered its head to the ground, making a ramp for Reagan to easily step down. "Good boy," she said as she patted its head.

General Gorum spoke up for the first time in quite a while. "Would the humans please join me up here?" He was standing next to King Andrew who was sitting on the throne.

"What about the dog?" Leo panted.

"Sure. You too, Leo," General Gorum said.

The girls all walked up and stood by the throne as General Gorum began his speech. "You were all very brave in the fight with the dragon. My goblins tell me that you used to use those pieces of Neon's horn for magic, including traveling back and forth from here to Earth. It isn't quite as good as Neon's horn, but I have something I want to give you."

General Gorum pulled the crown off his head and reached for what appeared to be a round, green orb in the center. He pulled it out and held it in the air. Liv didn't think it looked like anything very special.

For a crown gem, it wasn't even that pretty. It looked like a green, oversized marble. It was bigger than a marble but smaller than a golf ball.

"This has been in the Goblin Kingdom for thousands of years," General Gorum continued. "It can't be used for magic like Neon's horn pieces, but it will grant one wish per day—well, not just any wish. Actually, it's been around for so long that I can't remember exactly what it is supposed to do. I never use it. However, this is the item my goblins used to travel to Earth and back when we stole those horn pieces, so I know it will at least do that."

"No way! That's great!" Claire yelled.

General Gorum tossed the small, green gem to Liv, and she caught it.

"We might as well test this thing out right now," Liv said. "We've got to get home for dinner. How does it work?"

"Close your eyes, and wish you were home," General Gorum said. "Have your friends hang on tightly."

"I'll be back soon!" Reagan yelled to George.

"We'll come back next Saturday. I'll bring more Cheetos!" Claire hollered to King Andrew.

"And we'll be ready to help rebuild," Ava said.

Ava, Claire, Grace, and Reagan all grabbed Liv's arm. Leo ran over and nuzzled Liv's leg. Liv closed her eyes and wished she was home. She felt a rush of air as if she were starting to fly, but in an instant, her feet landed back on the ground. She looked around, and they were all standing in her backyard again. Leo started barking instead of talking, which always made Liv feel a tiny bit sad. She liked it better when he could talk. The sliding door on their deck opened, and their mom yelled, "Girls, your friends need to head home. It's dinnertime!"

Just in time, Liv thought to herself. She noticed that Reagan was standing with a blank stare on her face and her mouth hanging open.

"Pretty cool, right?" Grace asked her.

Reagan snapped back to reality. "I have a pet dragon. That is the coolest thing *ever*!" Reagan exclaimed.

"No, that was the coolest thing ever so far," Liv said, smiling. She looked down at the green orb in her hand that had just brought them back home. She already couldn't wait until next weekend when they could go back to the Unicorn Kingdom to help their friends rebuild their village.

The sliding door opened again, and their dad yelled to them, "Nobody gets a bite of food until your rooms are clean. Liv and Ava, your room is a disaster!"

Liv had completely forgotten that the goblins had torn their room apart the night before. "Looks like we have one more job to do before we can have some food," Liv said to Ava. "Once we get our room put back together, we need to find a better hiding spot for this thing." Liv then took another look at their new, green goblin orb.

"You're in on the secret now, Reagan," Grace said excitedly. "As long as you don't tell anyone, you can come back with us every Saturday to visit George. Who knows what will happen next time!"

ACKNOWLEDGEMENTS

There are almost too many people to thank that have helped me along the way with this book, but I'll take a stab at it. First off, I need to thank my loving and patient wife, Ali. Thank you for letting me continue to pursue writing amongst all the other chaos we have with the four kids. Thank you to Liv, Ava, Claire, and Mason for being such great listeners as I continue to make up crazy bedtime stories for you. Thank you as always, to my inner circle of secret readers (you know who you are!). Thank you to Padre for always being willing to be my first proof reader. Thank you to my team at Clay Bridges Press – Meg, Sarah, Alisa, and John – you guys are amazing. Thank you to my Republic Services family for being so supportive along the way. And last, but certainly not least – thank you to all of our dedicated readers. We wouldn't be able to do this without each and every one of you!

ABOUT THE AUTHOR

Kyle Rawleigh was born in the Twin Cities area of Minnesota. He lives there with his wife, three daughters, and one son. He still enjoys his day job working for a garbage company. When he isn't working, he can be found spending time with his family, being outdoors, cooking, and making up fun stories about unicorns to share with his children. Follow Kyle and his family on Facebook, Instagram, and Twitter @cotukstories.

Saving the King! Book 1: Chronicles of the Unicorn Kingdom

When three young girls who are living a very normal life in Minnesota try to find a way to save their dog, they find themselves in a very not normal situation. After some odd advice from their unicorn-crazed friend, they end up two worlds away following a unicorn who can barely remember his own name. With a lot of humor, courage, and a bit of magic, they set out to save their dog but wind up leading a revolution to save a world they never knew existed.